Spark Bird

This is one book from *The Ternion*, a series of novels published in 2024 under the #antiwrimo moniker. Please indulge in the others from the collection:

Julie, or Sylvia

Nicole Tallman, Ibrahim Sofiyullaha, Beryl Cooper
ISBN-13: 979-8-9895422-4-6

Escaping Emily

David Estringel, Alexandra Naughton, Risha Mae Ordas
ISBN-13: 979-8-9895422-3-9

SPARK BIRD

Jonathan Koven
Daniel DeRock
Julian Shendelman

A Novel

An #antiwrimo Book
Thirty West Publishing House

Spark Bird

ISBN-13: 979-8-9895422-5-3
Cover art by Jenn Zed
Jacket design by Josh Dale
Edited by Kat Giordano & Josh Dale
Printed in the U.S.A.

For more titles and inquiries, please visit:
www.thirtywestph.com

"Deserve your dream."

— Octavio Paz

Chapters

Nothing Here Can Hurt You

Simón reached Echo Bend Park, panting from exertion. The birdwatching group had already gathered at the trailhead. After a seven-mile ride from Saint Pluvia, a chill charged his glossed limbs. Overhead, the sumacs yawned, stretching red wings. A gust carried the newborn cold. Pinned to the daytime sky, a full moon leered beyond clouds, watchful as a nurse. Had he truly slept through summer?

Locking his bike to a fence, he scanned the group. Chanda was nowhere to be found.

It'd been stupid to come, though it was nice of her to pressure him out of his apartment. Simón felt absurd lugging along his heavy equipment. He was ready to return home when Chanda arrived.

Arms outstretched, she looked like a birding professional in a pine-green parka and matching pants. Healthy and well-rested to Simón's gaunt and gangly exhaustion, she embraced him.

In her arms, he felt displaced. Time had not only progressed in his months shut out from the world but switched tracks entirely. Disorientation swept in mists: the smell of too-soon September, the uncanny absence of walls, the peculiar nearness of strangers' faces — of Chanda's.

"Brought your gear, I see." She pointed to the black bag dangling from his shoulder.

"Thought I'd get back into it." He glanced at the others gathered up ahead, an eclectic dozen or so ranging from twenty-somethings to the obligatory retirees, binoculars slung from their necks. "Is it weird if I record?"

Chanda squinted, scanning his face. He braced for her usual teasing, but it never materialized. "No," she said. "I'm just surprised you'd want to. I mean, after everything."

The trail squished beneath Simón's mud-splattered canvas shoes. Every rock jabbed into his thin soles. He didn't mind, too preoccupied with the ash, the oak, the pine, and an incredible willow presiding atop a hill. All vibrantly undefeated, despite the leaves' gold-gilded rims. The foxglove and beebalm had only begun to pale.

He left Chanda talking to a retiree at the front of the group and slipped a few paces behind. Letting others pass, he smiled in a way that foreclosed conversation. Being around people was good for him; he knew that. It was just a lot.

Someone pointed halfway up a massive pine standing a few paces down the gentle hill. A gray and red bird perched on a branch, singing. Simón didn't know the name.

The watchers peered through binoculars, attached zoom lenses to cameras. The elderly man in front of Simón almost shook with excitement.

There were hundreds, maybe thousands of other, more compelling birds in the park. Simón closed his eyes and tuned his hearing to a distant, different bird whose song cut across all the others. Within moments, the group vanished around a curve in the trail. Not even Chanda had noticed he was lost in his own world.

Raindrops. The distant voices of the group faded into the wind's brash. Simón clutched the unified crescendo like a private treasure. When the bird's melody returned, it sounded a pitch higher, as though rising with each flutter of wings.

The warble was warm honey. Trembling at first, it bound tight, spooling into a slower rhythm. Three times, it repeated before splitting into a five-note measure. Simón etched the soundwaves in his mind, estimating frequency and amplitude, imagining how he'd isolate the song from the rustle of boots, rain's patter on leaves. Or, even better, how he'd slow the birdsong, loop it, add reverb, layer it over chiming creek water, breaking glass, laughing kids — how he'd construct a universe of vibrations plucked from the air.

Simón pulled on his headphones and set the recorder's gain. He lifted the shock mount of his mic toward the chirping, then clicked Record. Steadying the mount with his other arm, he waited for the bounding peaks uttered by the delicate voyager above — a combination of notes that might carry him, music that might save a life. The display's meter sprung and fell, blood rushing in and out of veins. He dared not make a sound. The recorder's red bar pulsed with patterned lyrics. He set the decibel level and removed his worn black headphones, determined to stay present.

Then, a shattering. Thunder so unearthly it seemed to electrify the world. Everything from the treetops to the falling rain shuddered violent red, igniting his head and spine. He was unhurt but overcome. A strange fire hummed through him. His hands and ears grew numb with cold, but the rest of his body scorched like a suppressed scream. He was shivering — but hot all over.

Am I nervous? Why am I nervous?

The clouds above Echo Bend broke. The wind stilled and the rain lifted. Sunbeams lanced the stress lines across Simón's forehead, and finally, he relaxed.

He directed his eyes to the infinite, listening, listening. Only the rustle of leaves. Perhaps the bird in question took off with the wind.

Gathering his equipment, Simón continued briskly along the pine-flanked trail, guided by an echoing variation of the same theme. Tracking its call, he veered off the trail into the bayberry shrubs, over aster beds and seeping moss, disregarding the thorned circuitry of ivy, the jagged faces of nettle leaves. He passed into another clearing.

He repeated the routine. Headphones on ears. Strong grip on shock mount. Microphone heavenward. Button tapped, level set.

Again, croaks of thunder sounded overhead, and rain swept the clearing.

He texted Chanda. *Rain, rain, go away.*

Gowns of sunlit rain blew from pine to pine, iridescent waves lashing around him. Lightning struck thick dark clouds above the park's entrance.

Again, the bird absconded. That would be it for the session.

Sleep taunted from his quiet, world-proof apartment. He sighed. No matter how deep, how pulsing the urge was to create, he was drawn, magnetic, toward surrender.

His phone buzzed with Chanda's response. *Not raining by us??*

He scrolled up, realizing she'd already messaged him twice asking where he was. In came another text: *OMW to the cafe. See you there?*

The time displayed on the rain-spattered phone screen was unexpectedly late. Had it really been over an hour? *It doesn't feel like it's been that long. And how is it not raining by her? Micro-micro-climates?*

More thunder, then lightning.

Simón pocketed the phone and set off to meet her. He'd have to wait to play back the recording. It was probably nothing special, but a seductive possibility remained.

Kittenville Cafe hummed with fluorescence and murmuring birders evaluating the morning's venture. Sleek cats wove between calves, bright eyes fixated on fishy treats. A round tabby sniffed at Simón's wet tube socks and grimaced.

On the bench beside him, Chanda strained to maintain a conversation with a purple-haired woman in a nearby armchair.

"—and Marlene's spark bird was the northern cardinal; she said it looked just like her Uncle Murray, red cowlick and all."

"Is Marlene your partner?" Chanda asked. She wore the pinched smile Simón recognized from their New Harbor University days, a mask applied when humoring someone she didn't like. It was more convincing now; years of nonprofit fundraising had honed her ability to prolong necessary conversations.

"Wife. We were married almost ten years." The woman frowned and sipped her kratom leaf tea, batting multiple little white paws away from the mug's rim.

"I'm sorry for your loss," Simón offered.

"Oh, she's not dead," the woman clarified, sweeping her hair behind her ear. "She left me for a safari guide. Said all my passions were child's play." She scoffed and shook her head. "Does this look like child's play to you?" The woman reached into her satchel and retrieved a spiral-bound notebook with Tweety Bird emblazoned on its warped plastic cover, then paused thoughtfully. "I guess it may have also had something to do with my research interests."

Even socially limber Chanda didn't know how to respond. She made anxious eye contact with Simón.

"What's a spark bird?" he asked, taking the hint.

"The first one that draws you into the lifestyle," the

woman said, happily pivoting topics. "For some it's a gorgeous, unusual bird, you know, like a peacock or a snowy owl. Mine's a red-tailed hawk. They're common but their call is beyond transcendental." She shook her head in amazement. "Too bad they've been dying en masse. I bet it's pesticides. Or chemtrails."

"Mine was a blue rock pigeon," interjected Chanda, fighting to keep the conversation on track. "My baba kept dozens in cages on the roof of his house in Old Delhi — he had ones with long necks or fuzzy feet or splashes of black feathers. Racing pigeons, some rare and expensive. But down on the street, outside his cages, there were blue rock pigeons. Pretty similar to the pigeons here — mostly gray, kinda pearly around the collar. They're fuckin' everywhere."

"Yeah, because they're invasive," the woman said.

"I'm *aware*," Chanda said. "But they're my spark bird all the same." She turned to Simón. "You'll find yours soon enough."

He took a big swallow of chamomile tea, the cheapest and smallest cup on the menu. "I might have already."

"Today?"

He nodded.

"What did it look like?"

"I couldn't see it — too high up, too many branches in the way. But I heard it. It was..." He shook his head, at a loss for words, just as the purple-haired woman had moments earlier. "Otherworldly," he said at last.

There was no way to describe the feeling without

sounding absurd. Even among these enthusiasts of the obscure, Simón worried about making himself look any weirder than he had by showing up to a birding event sans binoculars.

Simón dropped to a whisper and leaned closer to Chanda. "Don't you think it's a little weird that we're debriefing in a cat cafe?"

He hadn't been quiet enough.

"It's a rotten stereotype that bird lovers hate cats," the purple-haired woman said. "We're animal lovers for chrissake! These little guys were rightfully worshiped in the good ol' days. They're wiser and definitely closer to spiritual enlightenment than us *planet-killers*. Isn't that right, Jiggles?" She stroked the back of the fat tabby that had rejected Simón. "Cats should be the dominant species. The real problem is *people*."

He nodded, resonating with the sentiment. It was *people* who had derailed his career, *people* who had demanded he set aside art for science, *people* who believed they could dominate the natural world. The hubris of it all.

He glanced at his watch. He'd promised Chanda that he'd make a sincere effort to socialize for at least thirty minutes. But somehow, only fifteen had eclipsed since his arrival at the cafe. The remaining time dragged by, lethargic as the mountain of fluff passed out on the scratching board. He attempted to pick up the scowling, snub-nosed cat but was met with a flurry of claws. The sudden yowl sent every cat in the room scrambling and drew every human's attention. The birders laughed good-naturedly, but Simón couldn't bear it. Red-faced, he gathered his equipment and apologized profusely to an irritated Chanda before ducking out of the cafe.

⸻

The late afternoon light was gold and pink, almost warm. A rainbow searched the sky, consoling.

Behind Simón, the cafe door scuffed open, then closed. Footsteps chased after him. Chanda's hand gripped his shoulder from behind.

"You could've at least waited for me. I almost got stuck in another one of Roberta's stories."

Simón turned, guilty. "Sorry. Roberta?"

"Red-tailed hawk lady. She's harmless, as far as I know, but goddamn is she weird."

"Yeah." Simón scratched his scalp through tangled, oily hair. "Didn't mean to bail on you. It's getting late, and—"

"And you have so many pressing things to do, of course." Chanda jabbed a finger into his collarbone.

"Ouch. As a matter of fact, I do have plans."

"Let me give you a ride."

He shook his head, lips stretched into a thin smile. "My bike won't fit in your car."

Chanda shrugged. "I've got bungee cords."

He bounced on his heels. "I feel better, honest. Plus, the bike ride will be good for me." He knew she wouldn't argue with that.

"I *told* you birding would help. You gotta start listening to me more. I'm, like, really smart."

"You do have the occasional good idea." He looked away, wedging his hands into his pockets.

They hugged, Chanda pressing into the meat of his back. As she wandered toward her car, Simón adjusted his heavy gear bag and followed the sidewalk around the cafe.

But there was no bike. Only his chain dangled from the green metal fence, snipped. A whirlwind spun in the space behind his ribcage.

He ran toward the road, as if no chance remained of finding the bike thief. Even if he'd found them — then what? He slammed his palm against the brick exterior. The sting shot up his arm, into his clenched jaw.

It's just a bike. No big deal. You can get a new one.

But it'd been more than a bike. A sleek, gorgeous specimen, it was his only means of transportation, a perk from the old job and, until now, the only tether to his former self. The truth was, he couldn't afford a new one despite selling his shitty car a couple months back. His fingernails pinched into his palms.

Breathe. Nothing here can hurt you.

He moved to the maple tree beside the fence, pushed his weight against it, closed his eyes, and fell into his practiced meditation: spine straight, inhale naturally, exhale fully, and believe in Abi's words.

❧

The long walk home wound through Echo Bend Township before reaching the Redundo River Bridge. Golden hour shimmered across Saint Pluvia's skyscrapers as Simón crossed, hand tucked into his gear bag, fiddling with the recorder dials. Western winds thrust at his body as car after car throttled past. A sixteen-wheeler boomed its horn, but he was unfazed. The memory of the strange storm back at the park lifted him above the bridge and its traffic, over the rocky Redundo thrashing beneath.

He walked the rutted shoulder of the highway exit, past Saint Pluvia's outskirts, through the graffitied underpass, and down Cricket Avenue, the rowdiest drag of the city. One side was peppered with high-end gyms, açaí shops, psychedelic cafes, and art galleries; on the other side, people slept in battered tents and asked passersby for change. Simón wasn't afraid of being approached — as a child, he'd spent a few months living in a shelter with Ma, after Dad left — but he dreaded the guilt of having nothing to spare.

He wondered about the increasing breadth of the encampment; at least a hundred tents now, many times over what it'd been the year prior. It was the same throughout the city, as rents soared. He crossed the street, walked another mile, past the local pub and the shuttered vape store he'd frequented in the early days of his isolation, and then turned onto Butterfly Street.

The infamous Butterfly sinkhole seemed even bigger than it was months ago, when he'd last ventured this far from his apartment. He stood at the chain-link fence gating off the earthen fissure, gazing into its green-ringed depths, an esophagus holding Simón's name in its throat. But there was no light to see inside, no sound to be heard. He tossed a pebble through the fence. It tumbled, silent, into the chasm.

The apartment door creaked open and Simón was hit with a damp algal smell. The recording was burning a hole in his gear bag. There had been something electric in the bird's song, both familiar and strange. So much noise so quickly — rain, thunder, wind. But the call was a hot knife. He ached to dissect the track, to isolate the call, untangling the audio like a filthy apartment, disposing of empty bottles and crumpled wrappers, wiping away stubborn debris to expose the beautiful, rigid orderliness beneath.

But first, he needed to clean. He opened a fresh bottle of bottom shelf wine, filled a glass to the rim, and gulped it down before taking off his shoes or setting down the gear.

The coffee table was littered with half-eaten bags of snacks, purple-stained glasses and mugs from days, weeks prior; Miles Davis's autobiography, Julien Gracq's *Balcony in the Forest,* a book on audio mixing, all unread atop constellations of ground weed crumbs. By the table, the emerald couch cushion was embedded with the shape of his body. Dust engulfed every surface: the kitchen table (a cemetery for dirty plates), the television, the fridge door, the headboard, the bathroom mirrors, every wall, everywhere except his open laptop screen.

Music. He couldn't clean without music.

Lifting a record onto the turntable, an idea came to him. He slipped *The Tired Sounds of Stars of the Lid* back into its sleeve, fired up his laptop on the coffee table, and plugged in the field recorder. A few clicks and a long strip of green soundwaves glowed on the editing software interface. He set the track to loop, synced up his wireless speakers, and pressed play.

The raw, unedited recording sounded cleaner than expected. Some wind against the microphone, the rustling of shoes on dirt and leaves. Above all that, the birdsong.

Simón flung open the sets of curtains hiding the big glass balcony door and the windows behind the TV. North of his apartment, the horned skulls of industry reigned Saint Pluvia's throne; even the brilliant upper east-side foliage couldn't obscure the telecom and petrochemical towers. Despite the hour, there was still enough daylight to arouse the apartment. With the world's dying shine pouring in and the bird's trill and warble engulfing the soundscape, the apartment gradually transformed.

Invigorated by the soundtrack, Simón swiftly ripped the sheets off his bed and tossed them onto an already-full hamper, gathered mounds into the laundry machine, piled stray dishes. He even dusted with a stray sock slipped over his hand, like his mother used to do.

He took a well-deserved wine break. The reassuring

warmth trickled into his gut. From the speakers, a two-note pattern: low, then high and accented. It could have been his name, with some imagination. *Si – Món, Si – Món.* He harmonized, singing along with his name every time the bird cried out.

The track reached the end, then looped back. He froze, mid-sip, listening intently. There was something new in the recording that he hadn't heard the first time, or at least not consciously. His name. Not just the two-note pattern that vaguely resembled his name, but truly, albeit blurrily, his actual name. He stumbled, set the glass down. Turning back to the laptop, he examined the unremarkable waveform.

The song continued. He peered through the door's peephole, wondering if Chanda had followed him home. Maybe she was calling his name out in the hallway. But nobody was there.

He returned to the laptop. Maybe she'd called his name in the woods while searching for him and he hadn't even noticed.

He opened his editing software. First, he reduced the background noise. Studying the frequency, he noticed a recurring low rumble. A plane flying overhead, no doubt, though he didn't remember hearing one. Simón skipped through the track until he came upon the two-note pattern. He highlighted and copied that section, dropped it into another window. But it wasn't just one chirp, he realized. There was the two-note pattern, and beneath, a shadow of the very same sound, only several octaves lower. His stomach fluttered. He skipped ahead to the next iteration of that two-note pattern and repeated the process. Again, a shadow hiding in the lower frequencies. Simón adjusted the balance until the shadow notes came into focus and drowned out the higher chirps. A voice called from the speakers. Now it was unmistakable, calling over and over, each time more urgent; not the voice of someone in danger but someone searching, combing through dark woods. Searching for him.

Astounded, Simón dragged himself to the kitchen to refill his wine glass. He carried the sloshing vessel onto the balcony and gazed at the maroon skyline. In the distance, a few of the corporate towers had dimmed their lights, but not the Innovore building. Out further, green airplane lights twinkling behind dusk's mask.

He would go back inside soon enough. But until then, he would listen to the voice call out to him. The voice, a shadow in a bird's song.

Animal Sleep

i-món... Si-mó-ón...

The camera fixed on Simón.

Abi sang his name to him like it was music by itself. White sheets wrapped his happiness tight around him like a sanctum. Ma was there, Dad too, whispering to each other, frowns on their faces.

This was long before Abi left the family for good.

Simón reached a small hand out and found the brim of his grandfather's flat cap. The hat fell with Simón's grip and landed soft on his chest.

"Abi," he whispered. Though he could finally speak, 'abuelo' was still too much of a challenge, and the name stuck. "Abi-i-i."

A fantastic grin spread across Abi's face, like he'd glimpsed the first dawn after centuries of darkness. He turned toward Ma and Dad. "Mira, mira. He's singing."

Simón gazed through the window on the wall near the bed, one of his favorite things to do. Tonight, it rained. The sky was the color of cantaloupes. The moon, a scythe for kite strings. A gecko darted on the pane in a halfhearted attempt at entering through the glass, then chased away into the garden. Simón listened to the slur of rain, the patter, the gush — the rinsing, rinsing, rinsing of coral-colored waters. "Abi-i-i," he said again.

"Do you hear it? Your boy's singing!"

Ma finally spoke up while fighting with Dad. "Oh, stop it. That's not singing; that's just mimicking."

Abi turned his camera toward Ma and Dad for the first time, but Ma put her hand up at the lens.

"Enough. Pa, stop. STOP."

There was some fumbling before the camera returned to Simón, watching rainfall in the softly lit window. Slow, his eyelids shut, and the camera flicked off.

Simón didn't know why this memory returned so often. It was captured on tape, perhaps why it had cemented so clearly. Even so, he'd started reminiscing constantly about the days when he was too young to make decisions. Childhood felt like a scattered puzzle, ripe for reassembly.

He remembered how Ma and Abi would sit at the kitchen table and argue for hours in Spanish, some evidently personal matter. Though he only spoke English, his father's language, familiar Spanish phrases — *tu madre; me duele; porque no* — and his tía's name — *Cecilia* — wove through. He'd listen from his bedroom, following along as best he could with her cadences, absorbing the winding rivers of her sentences, the punctuation of her syllables, the rhythm of pauses between words he didn't understand.

Without Abi, Simón heard Spanish less and less often until even those few phrases evaporated. Ma fixed her focus even more intently on her only child after that. Her unrelenting overinvolvement in his schooling had landed him on the gifted and talented track. Whatever he showed interest in, Ma had too under the guise of support, whether geography or video games. When he'd joined a youth swim team, she'd followed in his footsteps, tracking each of their best times on an ad hoc scoreboard she'd made out of masking tape on the fridge. He'd quit just a few weeks in, sick of competing with his own mother. The exception, of course, was art. Her distaste for it provided a window for him to exceed her capabilities.

Simón's undergraduate thesis had been awarded top honors at New Harbor University, leading to a partial scholarship to the school's experimental music graduate program, one of the best in the country. There, he'd begun composing an unperformable five-hour symphony, comprising animal and other environmental sounds among meditative loops of sampled orchestra. He'd even written and recorded original piano and guitar passages for the capstone project — mostly simple, basic chords, edited beyond recognition with delay. His mentor confessed she'd told a colleague about the work, who'd mentioned it to his spouse, who'd mentioned it to his employer: an endlessly wealthy "disruptor" with a vast portfolio of vanity projects in need of unscrupulous artists to serve as creative directors, researchers, and innovators. A job offer from Innovore materialized overnight. Simón's symphony now lived in pieces on a brick-like external hard-drive in the depths of his closet, unfinished and unforgotten. He still believed he'd return to it. One day.

Throughout his time at Innovore, Ma would ask how his music was going, a somewhat polite inquiry not to be mistaken for genuine interest in his practice: instead, another way to illuminate his incompetence.

If he was honest with himself, Simón took pleasure in unfinished projects, even more so unfinishable ones. Incompletion meant avoiding reception and critique. But, most importantly, it imbued the works with a sense of eternal life.

How long had it actually been? Why had he stopped making art? Not just sounds to be spooned into the algorithms he'd fed for five years. Really, it was Innovore's investors he'd fed, who'd gambled on a revolution in meteorological prediction through wildlife responses to minute changes in air pressure.

The Innovore contract was dozens of pages long, outlining various nondisclosure policies and intellectual property stipulations and, in a larger font, the many perks of signing on. Access to a complimentary employee cafeteria with menus curated by celebrity chefs, generous stipends for healthcare and retirement fund contributions, unlimited PTO, and sick leave. And of course, the bicycle.

Meticulous Japanese craftsmanship merged with sleek Danish design to form a feather-weight speed-machine, perfect for commuting between his apartment and Slug Avenue, where Innovore HQ towered over the city center. It had been delivered fully assembled to his fourth-floor apartment, a glossy red bow sagging from the handlebar. He glanced up and down the hallway, but the courier was nowhere to be found. A crisp white gift tag dangled from the buttery calfskin grips. *Thank you for joining Innovore in the fight against climate change.*

His first day lacked a proper orientation; no one was there to greet him, including Ansel, the CEO and founder who'd personally poached him. A contract-to-hire employee, he had only an email sent by his recruiter with a list of detailed instructions. In the lobby, he read it over on his phone: retrieve a badge ID, request a microphoned headset and company card, and get access to several online tools with names like Gopher Prism and Aquafunction Risk Software. There were other items on the list, but he wasn't sure what they meant, most of them acronyms and given without context, or context that gestured nothing toward his comprehension of them.

- BISAM
- IICTFCEA (Drew S. [with the curly hair], super team ambassador of the Reporting and Data Absorption Board will compose a strategic roadmap for this task)
- LOFWA
- Corp Discovery Channel Infrastructure (to be reclassified Unpublic Cloud Control due to structural misalignment in Refine Diligently 180x)

He wasn't sure if some of these were programs to install on his desktop, or real-life facets of the business.

Still, the freedom was exciting — to be trusted on his own without any onsite contact. Of course, Ansel worked in the building as well, but he was likely busy with more important matters than acting as a greeting party.

The halls glowed with natural light. Simón took his time completing most of the tasks on his list before finally finding a seat in the radiant, open space. In lieu of cubicles, the office was filled with long tables with side-by-side seating. But despite this "collaborative" open floor plan, nobody spoke to one another, each employee staring into the depths of their monitors or wandering off to reservable flex spaces to attend video meetings. Along the perimeter, managers sat in glass-walled private offices, the perfect vantage point for surveilling their direct reports.

At the end of the day, he crossed the cloud bridge on the twentieth floor and reported to Ansel's palatial suite in the neighboring tech center, as per the recruiter's instructions.

"Were you able to get your company laptop up and running?"

Simón nodded.

"And do you have everything you need to get started?"

"I think so. Only..."

"Whatever you need, just ask."

"I was kind of hoping for some noise-canceling headphones. It's kind of hard to focus out there, with all the typing and stuff. I don't mean to sound ungrateful. The headset I got from HR isn't bad, but—"

Ansel threw his head back laughing. "You don't understand how valuable you are to me. You can have the most expensive pair of headphones on the market. Hell, you can have two. But I can do a lot better than that."

Simón arched an eyebrow, intrigued.

"Let's get you a private office."

"I thought those were just for managers."

"They are. But I've got a little workaround that shouldn't piss anybody off. Don't worry, Simon. No one will even notice." It would not be the last time Ansel forgot to add the accent to Simón's name, uncorrected.

Ansel's workaround landed Simón in one of the tech center flex rooms, a space double the size of any individual manager's office with a sweeping view of Saint Pluvia. "I've set your 'room reservation' to auto-renew indefinitely," Ansel said. "You can have all the space you need to innovate. And don't hesitate to ask for anything else."

The next morning, an invisible facilities team had installed a sprawling workstation with a massive, curved monitor at the center, just above the laptop's docking port. A plush ergonomic chair and a pair of shiny thousand-dollar headphones awaited him.

The work was straightforward enough. Innovore flew Simón to a few dozen locales, armed with the finest equipment money could buy. A stranger would collect him at the airport before wordlessly driving Simón to a nearby nature preserve. He'd record animals in nature; mostly birds, sometimes insects, small mammals, whatever the biologists flagged as worthwhile. He failed to remember more than a handful of species names; he knew the basics — cardinal, woodpecker — but he wasn't paid to understand ornithology. If timed well, Simón would be on a return flight by nightfall. If not, the fixer would then drop him off at an airport hotel, where he'd burn through his per diem at the bar. Back at the office in Saint Pluvia, he'd comb through each audio file, tagging any noise and isolating the defining elements, editing them to perfection before dropping the file into a portal.

Working his way through a backlog of unedited recordings, intermixed with the mechanisms of Innovore's dull bureaucracy, consumed the first year. He settled in. The bright office offered a welcome respite from years of entitled coffee shop customers and hostile retail managers. The cafeteria was as delicious as the digital handbook had promised, and he soon regained the weight he'd lost as a starving student.

His editing work was both secretive and specialized, and Ansel was the only person with the security clearances to assess it. Though quirky — Ansel didn't eat so much as he gulped gray protein sludge from a gallon-sized jug — Simón found the CEO to be charming and appreciative, and, as a bonus, not bad to look at. He and Ansel had a standing monthly check-in, during which he would occupy Simón's chair and listen to each new edit. All the while, Simón would stand beside him in polite, impatient silence.

"Brilliant," Ansel would mutter, staring at the inscrutable valleys and peaks of an albatross' scream.

Simón wasn't sure what was brilliant about plugging sound files into pre-existing software and meticulously cleaning up the audio but accepted the affirmations all the same.

"You're seriously getting the hang of this."

"Thank you. But I'm not really doing anything. I'm just cleaning up the tracks. I'm not even sure what I'm supposed to be looking for."

"That's the algorithm's job. Once we have enough content in there, it'll map the weather patterns onto each track's characteristics and boom! We'll have the key to everything. If we can unlock the weather, we can save lives from natural disasters, we can optimize global trade routes, we can put an end to famine and drought. I mean, Simon, my friend, we're talking *real* disruption."

But as the months went on, Simón spent less time traveling and recording, and far more time rotting in endless, inscrutable meetings. Soon, most of his days were spent on-call. It seemed instead of actually working on tasks, they were discussed ad nauseam; how the tasks fit into an imaginary book of work, the associated risks and potential added value, the operational timeline juxtaposed against a pre-existing backlog. Before so much as an email could be sent, the details had to be proposed, workshopped, approved, finalized, and accounted for on the Work Board. And then, any progress that managed to eke by would be recounted in biweekly project management meetings. It was a culture of implication, posture posing as transparency.

The contract was extended again and again, but he was never hired full-time. Locked away like a private muse in his oversized private office, Simón found it impossible to make friends. He could feel the castigating burn of judgment of everyone who passed his door. He'd gotten close once; there'd been a woman at the holiday party who'd tipsily confessed her attraction to him. After a week of her batting her eyelashes at him in the elevator, they entered a perfectly utilitarian three-month relationship, which ended as soon as she found someone more like her. It was no great loss; the only music she liked came from Disney musicals. But aside from that fling, he hadn't connected with anyone. No one, except Ansel.

After five years of reliable monotony, Ansel appeared in Simón's office unannounced in a skintight Armani polo, days before their scheduled sync.

"I wanted to thank you," Ansel began. "You've made an incredible impact on Operation Birdsong, and at Innovore more generally." Ansel shifted in his chair with uncharacteristic apprehension, running his fingers through his preternaturally full hair. "Simon... May I be frank with you?"

Simón nodded, heartbeat quickening.

"I've built my empire off the creative energy of geniuses like you. I don't take that labor for granted. I know you've made sacrifices to be here, as have countless others. But," he sighed, gathering himself, "there are parts of my empire that, despite extensive investment and bottomless resources, lack the same... potential as Innovore's core income generating projects. At least, that's what my new financial advisor says."

"Maybe we can find a way to make this profitable," Simón said, desperation surging. "I could collaborate with a developer; we could make an app or something. Like 'Duolingo' for bird calls."

Ansel nodded patronizingly. "It's a brilliant idea," he said, glancing at his titanium smartwatch. "But Innovore is all about growth. We're all evolving, all the time. We were always going to outgrow each other. It's time to take on a new challenge; it's in your best interest."

There was no severance pay for contractors. Half of his final paycheck went to rent, the rest to assorted living expenses.

During his hibernation, Simón came to realize it wasn't entirely Ansel's vascular hand blotting out the sun, shutting him in a cocoon, draining his savings until he wondered how he'd make rent going forward — much less, student loan payments. He'd done it to himself, abandoning New Harbor's grad program to follow a trail of praise.

The first month of freedom had been productive and driven; he'd kept a tidy apartment and prepared budget-friendly meals. He regularly wandered to Nectar House off Butterfly Street, the local watering hole, for companionship. By the second month, his ambitious routines collapsed. Unbathed and underfed, he entered a monk-like state of gradual decay, the sharp edges of burnout blurring into a heavy opacity, begging for anesthetization in the solitude of his apartment. A gauzy film enveloped everything. Numbness was a relief.

Chanda texted and called. She even had her dweeby boyfriend Terrance message him. This final awkward intervention usually did the trick, yielding an economical *'Hey, sorry, I'm good.'* While his response kept Chanda temporarily at bay, the internal fissure only worsened.

Still, there were moments of sweetness in his glacial summer. As he drifted in and out of lucidity, long-forgotten memories resurfaced. The details were less important than their arrival — scattershot visions of Abi, displaced of all context — precious, mysterious gifts.

Lost in nostalgia, Simón was terrified when Chanda banged on his door for a wellness check, bumbling police officers in tow.

"What the fuck was I supposed to do? You wouldn't even answer Terrance!"

Chanda was pissed, but in his meditative, depressive state, Simón could see the fear beneath her fury. She took a few days to recover, then invited him to the birding meetup.

"You don't have to enjoy it," she said. "You just have to show up. It's good practice."

"For what?"

"For being a person again."

❧

Simón opened the curtains and squinted against the needling morning light. His dreams had been threaded with birdsong, and when unspooled, the melody led him down shifting corridors, stairways, tunnels. Always beyond reach.

Before bed, he'd extracted one-hundred-eighty seconds of the recordings in which the recitation of his name was clearest, emailing the file to Chanda without explanation. He'd waited impatiently for a response before realizing it was after midnight.

He waited as long as he could stand: 7:42 AM.

"Well? Did you listen?"

"It's very nice, Simón." She sounded busy, out of breath from walking at her typical breakneck pace.

"Nice? What'd you hear?"

"I think it's just a blue jay. Maybe an owl."

"Just a blue jay," he echoed.

Chanda's silence was heightened by the racket behind her — grinding, hammering, the occasional deep-voiced holler. "Are you okay?" she asked, at last.

"I'm good," he lied. "Where are you?"

"Actually, not far from your place. Just got off Butterfly Street. They're finally working on the sinkhole. I'm doing this month-long walk-to-work challenge. No way I'm letting that fucker from volunteer management beat me again."

Chanda's principled, resentful streak typically amused him, but he was distracted by what she hadn't heard in the recording. If she couldn't make out the obvious repetition of his name, then what did that say about his sanity? Maybe she'd been right to worry about his well-being. He'd been alone for a long time now.

"When's the next one?" he asked.

"What?"

"The birdwatching thing."

"Oh!" There was relief in her voice. "Next Sunday, same place and time. Meet you there?"

"Actually, I was hoping for a ride."

With little else to do (other than apply to jobs, a task he despised), Simón dipped out of the apartment early the next morning, gear bag weighing on his shoulder.

The sky glittered awake, and a warm wind sent red leaves tumbling over cracks in the pavement. Again, the visible moon lingered silver above the highest clouds.

Simón's block was about a mile from Saint Pluvia's industrial nave. Innovore's crystalline skyscrapers glinted with sunlight, patrolling the city like fiery-eyed sentinels mounted over the planet's edge. This morning, as Simón walked the blocks to Butterfly Street, the sky's reflection moved in the towers' glass windows.

Pigeons were always crashing into Innovore's windows, necks snapping on impact. The brutal weekly occurrence had brought raucous cheers and exaggerated applause from staff. He knew it was despicable, or ironic, at least, for a company that prided itself on environmentalism. Still, he'd be lying if he'd never rejoiced over a well-timed collision.

His fists curled, and he cracked every knuckle. *It's been over three months,* he thought. *Move on.*

By the corner of Butterfly and Cricket, the sinkhole waited for Simón's arrival. The perimeter had chipped away even further, its edges creeping closer and closer to the fence. A nearby crane sat dormant, and a bright blue tube dangled off the lip, presumably too short to drain whatever liquid lay within. It seemed like any and all progress had halted. He crept closer for a better look, pulling himself up and over the chain-link fence. Careful as he hopped off, he ensured his balance on the crust. His knees wobbled before the sinkhole.

The unseeable depths were more colorful up close, shades of pewter rippling to black, black to blue. Shifting hues, or maybe a puff of dust or smoke, it was hard to say. Strange indigo wildflowers grew on the sinkhole's greener ridges, dew on their petals. Soft, they quivered like the lips of a crying child. He leaned over the edge and a honeyed fragrance wafted up toward him, cool and warm at the same time. Then, a vague, purring echo. The asphalt beneath his feet began to bow.

"Freeze!"

Simón stumbled back, then turned toward the voice, heart pounding.

The face across the sinkhole smudged against the

magenta sunrise. A silhouette slipped out from behind the crane's bulky wheels.

Simón instinctively put his hands up. "I'm leaving. I was just curious, that's all."

As he turned to climb back over the fence, sunlight caught on purple hair.

"Wait." Simón strained his eyes. "Don't I know you?" It was hard to forget one of the only people he'd spoken to in months.

The woman stiffened, then ducked back behind the crane. Simón carefully scurried along the perimeter in pursuit.

"Red-tailed hawk," Simón yelled, the last word echoing off the surrounding brick and concrete.

At that, she turned, then laughed. "Of all the gin joints in all the world!" Roberta waved him over.

The street was still half-asleep, just a handful of early risers walking their dogs before work.

"What are you doing here?" he asked.

"I could ask the same."

Simón nodded. *Stalemate.*

"You know," Roberta said, "I thought you might jump."

He laughed and she glanced around, checking to see if anyone had heard.

"We'd better duck out before someone narcs."

Despite their height difference, Roberta had no trouble keeping pace with Simón as they sped away from the pit.

"What's got you out of the house this early?" Simón asked.

"Just clearing my mind before work. Where are you headed?" "The park. I meant to go straight there, but the hole…"

"Alluring, ain't it? There's something about an abyss that just—" She shivered with delight. "The endlessness!"

"Exactly," he marveled. "Hey, uh, weird question, but did you hear anything when we were over there? Like the sound of a drill?"

She shook her head. "But I'll be the first to tell you that sound is a personal experience. After my wife left I kept hearing her dry little cough in every room of the house. My sister said I just missed her but sounds have an afterlife of their own."

Simón hesitated, assessing her trustworthiness. "You know how I was recording at the meetup last weekend?"

"Couldn't miss it. Not too many birders show up with a full podcast rig." She laughed. "I thought you were some kind of public radio dork. They love following us around. Get anything good?"

"Funny you should ask. There was something I couldn't identify."

"A bird?"

He nodded.

"And something else? Something suspicious?"

"I'm sure it was just a fluke. It was nothing."

Roberta stopped in her tracks, grabbing his arm. Her

eyes, flanked by crow's feet, pulsed with electricity. "If it was nothing," she said, her brassy voice suddenly velvet, "then why are you out again today at the crack of dawn with your equipment?"

Simón pulled away. "I'm just weird, that's all."

"Nothing wrong with being weird." She glanced at her phone. "I've gotta go set up my classroom before the kids get in. Will you be at the park this weekend?"

He nodded.

"Good. Bring that recording with you, plus whatever you manage to get today. Maybe I can help." And with that, Roberta marched toward Earhart High.

It was over an hour before Simón made it to Echo Bend Park. The closer he got, the more he regretted letting Roberta in on his secret. She was already too invested for his taste, which inexplicably made his jaw clench. By the time he arrived the source of his uneasiness rose to the surface; he had to remind himself that Roberta wasn't Ma. He set up his equipment, aiming the shotgun mic at the golden canopies overhead, then squatted, waiting. The park was boisterous — caws and cries, chirps and chatter, an entire ecosystem of sound. The sun crept higher. His thighs cramped and he shifted onto the seat of his pants, unbothered by the moist dirt. His gut churned, having forgotten to eat earlier. Stubborn human body, always crying out for nourishment. He'd been foolish to believe he could just show up and find the same bird in the same place; it probably didn't have a nest there, just passing through on its way south for the winter. The original recording was probably a delusion sparked by prolonged isolation, an unconscious craving to peel back a chirp to its psychic kernel, to know his name as its nucleus. An hour of wasted space on his SD card for nothing.

Just as his finger brushed the STOP button, melody blanketed him like a lightning storm, trembling and spooling, trembling, and spooling. An aria of five notes. And then, nothing. Its electricity surged through him, left him overheated, drenched in sweat. He touched the back of his neck, then stared at his glistening palm. Whether it was another delusion or a miracle, he would decide to go back home after analyzing the recording.

He left Echo Bend Park, past the visitor pavilion and through the lot, which swarmed with incoming professional dog walkers and spandex-clad parents pushing jogging strollers. He narrowly avoided a biker, who blasted a sped-up pop song with chipmunk vocals from cheap speakers. He passed the vandalized port-a-potties, the weeping willow, a gaggle of geese being harassed by a toddler, a cluster of teenage missionaries in neckties passing out pamphlets at the bus stop. He walked uphill into a mixed-income neighborhood of pastel-roofed houses. Cars, a mix of new all-electric models and beaten down gas-powered sedans, were parked on both sides of the leafy street.

He trekked past the refuge of suburbia, out onto the turnpike's bustle, walking along the shoulder. He cursed himself for selling his car and for losing his bike. Even the bus felt like an impossible luxury these days. He hadn't used his muscles like this in months — shoulders, back, legs, hips, feet, all pulsing and burning.

Five miles remained. He stopped, opening every pocket and zipper of his gear bag for forgotten medicine. He grazed a disposable cannabis vape leftover from his commuting days. He'd managed to get by on wine alone for the last few days, but the pain had pushed him over the edge.

It tasted like artificial cherry and diesel fuel. The specter of his smoke vanished in the wind.

He entered an underpass preceded by a cartoon billboard, which portrayed a pink-spotted beetle being sprayed by insecticide: the advertised product. There had been a sudden boom in the invasive population, subsuming the state's ecosystem. Simón didn't know much else about it, but there had been a public notice to neutralize the beetles on sight. The cartoon's text read, *Burn every last one of them!*

"Jesus," Simón muttered. It occurred to him that, just a week earlier, he wouldn't have thought twice about the billboard. Now, his foggy brain spun a web that linked the mass influx of famished beetles to the blistering summer, to the rising seas that threatened New Harbor's coastline.

He crossed the bustling bridge, all the while attempting to unclog the vape, which had stopped pulling smoothly. Hungry for another clean hit, he sucked it like a vacuum when a voice called out from a sheet of flattened cardboard.

"Help the homeless?" the elderly woman asked.

"I'm sorry," Simón said, lowering the pen from his mouth. "I don't have anything. Honest."

His phone buzzed and he quickly glanced at it before pocketing it. A text message from Chanda: *Did I just see you walking Redundo Bridge??*

"Nothing?"

"No, I'm sorry. I really don't."

"What about some of that — that thing you got there." The bony, sunburnt woman pointed to his hand. "Just one hit? One little *fff! —pahhh*?" She mimed blowing smoke from her chapped lips.

"It's— I don't—" The woman looked sickly, and he wondered if sharing would do her more harm than good. "Not today, sorry."

To look into her eyes would have meant acknowledging the ugliness of his refusal. He failed to avert his gaze — her irises gray as the Redundo River. Breaking free from their grasp, he forged ahead.

Her shout belted across traffic. "You're selfish! You're a selfish young man!"

The rest of the mile-long walk down Cricket grew cold. His mouth went dry. Every few moments brought the nagging feeling he'd dropped something important. Eventually, the sensation overwhelmed him. He emptied his bag onto someone's raised garden bed and surveyed the contents: the mic and its mount, the recorder with its case, headphones, several stray wrappers, and coins, an unused Innovore koozie, a near-empty water bottle, a journal, and a few writing utensils. It was all there. He sighed at his paranoia, gathered his possessions, and continued, anxious to be home.

At the intersection of Cricket and Butterfly, a police car and ambulance with flashing lights sat beside a gathering crowd. Kids and their parents surrounded the sinkhole, presumably killing time while waiting for a school bus delayed by the commotion. The fence was ringed with caution tape.

Simón licked his desiccated lips, then approached a bearded man wearing tie-dye pajamas.

"What happened? I live a few blocks down," Simón said, as if to justify his intrusion.

"Ay. Yeah, they think someone fell in."

Simón's eyes widened. "In the hole?"

"Late last night," the man continued. "Somebody reported it, though I'm hoping it's just a raccoon or possum. There are way cooler ways to die than in a damn hole."

Simón considered this. Death by sinkhole was far more appealing than rotting away on his sofa. The cavity fascinated him. How strange to be pulled by unknowable forces. Wasn't that the definition of inspiration? The draw of the unseen?

In a trance, Simón drifted back to the apartment. Inside, he slipped off his shoes, bag, and jacket, fighting to stay alert long enough to listen to the new recording.

The only thing he'd consumed that day was a room-temp Coke Zero, the last of dozens pilfered before departing

Innovore. He extracted a freezer-burned bagel from behind a frosty fifth of cheap vodka to toast and slather with store brand peanut butter. While chewing, he uploaded the morning's capture, then pressed play. Warbling birdsong rang out, unimpeded by background noise. He listened carefully for another auditory shadow.

Leap from...

The voice was less hidden this time. His heart pounded. He tracked back a few seconds, praying to hear it again.

Leap from the...

The rest of the message was fuzzy. He selected the section of the track with the utterance, plus a few seconds after he suspected the message ended, to be sure. He then copied and pasted the section into a new pane and worked on it.

Leap from the cloud bridge. The words rang out rich and clear, on repeat. *Leap from the cloud bridge. Leap from the cloud bridge.*

Shadow of a Song

Easy, he slipped right back into his chemical routine. His whole body was sore from miles of walking, and he was out of Advil; it was as good a reason as any.

On the living room couch, he ground a dry nug of weed, one of the last in his dwindling stash, and packed it into a murky glass bowl.

His muscles melted, but his head was still swimming in circles around the latest message. He retrieved a Xanax from the bottle on the kitchen counter, washing it down with a gulp of flat cola before flopping into bed. He stared at the white stucco ceiling for an incalculably long time.

The pill hadn't been able to push the message away. But now he could observe its impact from a safe distance, rotate the message, study it, break it down into graspable pieces.

Cloud bridge.

Nearly every weekday morning for five years, he'd walked across the cloud bridge. Encased in transparent glass and reinforced with sleek silver beams, the bridge connected Innovore's towers, forming an uppercase H in St. Pluvia's skyline.

Simón could feel himself gripping a branded travel mug filled with complimentary fair trade coffee, Slug Avenue's traffic churning twenty floors below. The acute pounding of a pigeon against the glass.

Sleep massaged its way up his body. *Leap.* In waking dream, the cloud bridge's glass panels shattered; wild winds clawing him, beckoning. *Leap.* Exhaustion pressed down on his face like a heavy blanket, a pleasant smothering. The whipping wind slowed and warmed.

No longer hovering in the liminal space between Innovore's towers, Simón found himself on a swinging rope bridge.

The pungent scent of orangutans and tropical birds washed over him. Spider monkeys played and rested in the tall canopies and low basins of a man-made habitat. His uncalloused hands could barely wrap around the fat jute cord as he stared down at Abi's extended arms.

He'd been watching the spider monkeys all day, studying their graceful, fearless acrobatics. The whole time, Abi pointed to the drains in the sand-colored floor, the green murals walling the enclosure, the cold fluorescence above.

Artifice, he'd said. *Do you know that word?*

Simón shook his head.

It means someone decided what was real, and what wasn't. It means nothing here can hurt you.

In his mother's telling, she had just returned from a trip to the restroom, catching up in time to see Simón wiggle through the bridge's vertical lengths of rope and leap toward Abi. Frozen halfway between horror and disbelief, her eyes traced his downward trajectory until he made cracking contact with the cement walking path.

But all Simón remembered was the ride to the hospital, a whirlwind of brilliant noise. Was there pain? The sensation was blurry, crowded out by the animal stink of the nearby enclosures.

Sometime later, in a white room, his arm was bundled and numb.

Was it your idea to jump or Abi's? Ma asked, every answer the wrong answer.

The cast would itch mercilessly for weeks. He stuck pencils, butter knives, and anything else he could find into the gap between cotton and skin, yearning for relief.

In this version of the story, the pencil slipped in and vanished. He peeled back the plaster edge, only to find a dark, impossibly deep void, a pit that swallowed him whole. Sucked into the depths of his own cast, Simón fell and fell and fell. Abi's words rang out like an alarm: *Nothing here can hurt you.* The descent, warm and welcoming.

Mid-day painted his eyelids through the bedroom window. On the floor, his phone vibrated on and on.

The next four days — Wednesday through Saturday — drifted by in a haze. As soon as the slightest tinge of sadness or anxiety resurfaced, Simón medicated it into submission. Scrolling through his news feed, he barely registered the reports of dead flocks of uninjured seagulls washing ashore on the coast, hordes of invasive, pink-spotted beetles destroying entire vineyards, unexpected seismic activity triggering evacuations from the area surrounding a supposedly extinct volcano a few states over. The broadcasts swirled together to form a surreal fog of disaster so pervasive as to be unconcerning.

Finally, in the wee hours of Sunday morning, he remembered his last call with Chanda and the agreement they'd made. He looked around at his depression pit, recognizing the physical manifestation of his despair. A nascent will to survive, a small wormy thing, cautiously poked its head above ground. *I'll start over in the morning,* he promised himself, taking one last Xanax to lull himself to sleep.

Upon waking, a bleary-eyed and newly sober Simón collected everything he needed for the meetup — apart from his wallet. He didn't want to waste the day's momentum looking for it and was sure Chanda would spot him at the cafe after, if needed. He stepped outside, recording equipment weighing on his shoulder. The blare of distant sirens, the onslaught of sun, the reek of fresh mulch, all hastened his headache. Fifteen minutes passed with no sign of Chanda. He was drafting a *Where are you???* text when he realized he hadn't listened to her voicemails. There were four from Wednesday alone, more in the days that followed.

Wednesday, 2:15 PM. Simón, I don't wanna see you walking on the turnpike anymore. You'll end up roadkill. If you're that hard up for money, you should just ask for help. I can't pay your rent, but I can certainly loan you bus fare.

Hell, call it a gift. Call me back.

Wednesday, 2:18 PM. Me again. I hope that didn't sound condescending. You know I respect you, right? If you feel— AACK.

The call ended with a shriek. Had she fallen into the sinkhole?

Wednesday, 2:33 PM. Okay, so I'm not sure when exactly the call disconnected, but I hope to god you heard the whole thing because absolutely nobody's gonna believe this shit. So, I'm walking around downtown leaving you voicemails, right? I'm yammering away under the cloud bridge when something hits me — an entire fucking pigeon! Its wing is pointing the wrong direction, and its beak is cracked, but that resilient motherfucker is alive! I think it hit the glass. Anyway, I put it in my tote bag. Call me back.

Simón pulled the phone from his ear and stared at it blankly. Cloud bridge. Hearing the words again put him off-balance, out-of-body. A pinprick of paranoia: had Chanda somehow known? He took a deep, ragged breath before listening to the next message.

Wednesday, 3:48 PM. Okay, so me and Picasso — get it? 'Cause he's all bent out of shape? — made it home without killing each other. I got him set up in the bathtub with a towel, a water dish, and some stale tortilla chips because I didn't have any seed laying around. The wildlife rehab place said they don't take pigeons at all. Some bullshit about how if they did, they wouldn't have space for any other type of animal. Monsters! But the vet down the block said I could bring him in tomorrow morning. Might be like two or three hundred to get him patched up. What is my life! Oh, and by the way, where the fuck are you? I'm gonna be pissed if you got hit by a car on the way home. Don't make me start calling hospitals.

Thursday, 9:13 AM. I drove by your place last night and saw all your lights on. So at least you're not dead. Maybe you were tired when you got home, so you took a bunch of black-market Adderall and spent the whole day and night in one of your little editing wormholes. I'm glad you're making art again, really. I just wish you'd communicate with me. I feel like a fucking ass calling you all the time knowing that you won't even listen to these messages. Anyway, just dropped off Picasso. I've got a few hours to kill before he's ready to get picked up. I kind of thought they'd just nurse him back to health there, but apparently they're gonna send him home with me? Guess I've got a new roommate. Terrance is gonna lose it.

Friday, 6:15 PM. Just got home from work, figured I'd try you again. Picasso is settling in okay, and Terrance hasn't dumped me, so things are working out. Bathroom smells pretty bad, gotta get some fresh newspaper to put down. Terrance says he won't shower here until Picasso gets a proper cage. But he's a free-range bird! I can't just shove him in a jail cell. Anyway, I'm a little full up on bird drama right now, so I can't take you to the meetup on Sunday. I slipped some bus money into your mailbox. Please — just text me so I know you haven't OD'd. It's stressing me the fuck out. If I don't hear from you by Monday, I'm calling the cops again. You don't even have to text me a full sentence. I'll take an emoji. Okay. Bye.

Simón deleted his half-written text and selected the dove holding an olive branch. Hopefully, it would symbolize her inevitable forgiveness for his negligence. After sending it, he hazily recalled a fact about doves being fancier pigeons and wondered if he'd unwittingly disrespected Chanda's precious patient.

He turned back to the building's entryway and carefully unlocked his overstuffed mailbox, using one hand to hold all the unpaid bills and insurance marketplace notifications in place and the other to extract the wad of crinkled bills wedged into the compartment's uppermost layer. There was easily thirty bucks in the clump, enough for ten trips with transfers.

The ride wasn't bad; this time on a Sunday, most people were either at home or in church. Crossing Redundo Bridge, the bus rocked, rear launching skyward as its tires passed over a pothole.

Everyone except Simón yelped.

He blinked, listening to his earbuds. Hiroshi Yoshimura's *Wetland* transmitted a vaporous, natural haze across his brain. His legs were restless as he stared out the windows into the river's gray-green thrash. A text came in from an unknown number.

hey dont come 2 park

Then, immediately, another.

its roberta got banned— asshole guard kicked me out. meet @ chili dog kingdom on Clover. lez eat. got ur # from Chanda btw, told me im ur chaperone lol. dont worry kid I got u.

His empty stomach churned at the idea of a chili dog, but he tugged the pull-cord at Clover all the same.

Chili Dog Kingdom was a few blocks down from the bus stop, next to a local pub and across from Toys 4 Us, a sex shop that, according to their signage, was premiering an erotic VR game that week. As he approached, he saw Roberta outside, waving her arms like she was directing an airplane on the tarmac.

Her hair, though still vibrant in hue, was disheveled. Bits of dry leaves mingled with pine needles in the ratted magenta mess. Her face was uncharacteristically bare.

"You would not believe the day I've had." She laughed, patting down her mane as Simón slid onto the fiberglass picnic bench across from her.

"Dare I ask?"

She sighed, pinching the bridge of her nose. "This is gonna sound worse than it actually is, okay?"

"Okay."

"Seriously, no judgment, please."

He threw up his hands as if to declare Chili Dog Kingdom a safe space.

"I may have... *lightly* kidnapped a child?"

"What?!"

"The short version is, I got to the park early so I could

use the workout equipment before the meetup. And all of sudden, I see a baby in a car seat, in the middle of an open field. There was nobody around, so I figured I'd turn her in. But the thing is, I couldn't find anybody. I start circling the park with the baby looking for a security guard."

"Why didn't you just call the police?"

She scoffed. "With my record? Yeah, right."

Simón didn't dare inquire further. "So, then what happened?"

"Some crazy man starts running at me. Fucking terrifying! I start running too, car seat in tow. I swerve into the bushes, but the kid's screaming too, so I can't even hide properly. The guy is getting closer, and then this airborne robo-cop barks orders to drop the baby. And I'm like, drop the baby?"

At this point, Simón wasn't buying it, but he played along.

"You didn't—"

"Of course I didn't drop the baby. I gently set the car seat down, and right then— thwack! A security guard pops out of the wood, tackles, and cuffs me. Turns out the crazy guy was just the baby's dad — how was I supposed to know? Anyways, they hauled me to their offices and perma-banned me from the park." Her shoulders sunk in defeat.

"But it was a misunderstanding, wasn't it? Couldn't you just tell them?"

"I did, trust me. But he was all, blah blah, you're the reason we had to get drones, blah, blah, this is your third strike. Anyway, that's why I had you meet me here."

If that was the short version of the story, Simón couldn't fathom what the long one entailed. "I wasn't really up for a hike anyway," he said.

"Hungover?" she asked.

"More or less."

"Yeah, you look like shit. Ain't we a pair?" She patted his hand. "So, let's hear it. The recordings!"

"Right, right," he said, rummaging through the bag at his side. He handed her the bulbous headphones. "This is from last week, at the meetup. I thought I heard—"

"Don't tell me yet," she said. "You'll bias the results."

He nodded and pressed play, awaiting some kind of reaction. At the twenty second mark, when the bird uttered his name, Roberta's eyebrows shot up to meet her hairline. She laid the headphones on the table and leaned in, whispering. "And you were totally alone, right? It's okay if you got confused. I get confused all the time."

"I'm positive," he said.

She exhaled forcefully and shook her head, perhaps in disbelief, or maybe abject horror. "You got more like this?"

"Yeah, I went back to the park, right after I saw you on Wednesday."

She put the headphones back on and nodded, signaling for him to play the clip. He cued up track two. Her eyes widened.

Simón leaned across the table. "So, you heard it. You actually heard it."

Roberta nodded slowly. "I think it's best if we change the subject." Her expression changed suddenly into a wide smile. It was alarming how fast that mask came on. "You should eat!"

Inside, a gray-haired man dunked onion rings into a sizzling fryer. It was a strange place to dine on a Sunday morning, this fluorescent-lit cavern beyond time and space. A small, humble restaurant, six green picnic tables cramped together in place of tables and chairs. A family with two young kids sat at one table. At another sat a group of early-twenty-somethings staring wordlessly into coffee cups, faces streaked with glitter, bloodshot eyes swirling with whatever chemicals had powered them through the long night. One wore the sex shop's proprietary VR goggles, and another was pleading for a turn. On one wall, a soda fountain. Covering the opposite wall, a poorly painted mural: a castle of cheese fries surrounded by a moat of steaming chili, a hot dog king perched atop, crown tipped to one side, winking, giving a thumbs-up.

He didn't want to eat chili. He wanted to talk about the message in the recording. But his stomach grumbled.

"You gotta try the King Dog — they add a layer of cheese fries."

His stomach twinged. "I'll probably just get a plain dog. And some orange juice," he said, the juice an empty gesture toward self-preservation.

"Suit yourself."

Roberta approached the register while Simón stood

back and searched again for his wallet. Not in the pocket of his jeans, not in his jacket, not in his gear bag. *Maybe it really is gone*, he thought. His mind jumped to the walk home, the weed pen, the homeless woman. Had he been so out of it that he'd been robbed by an old woman without noticing? *You're a selfish young man!* she shouted.

He pulled the crumpled wad of cash from his pocket and stared, unable to look away from it. Until he got his wallet back or replaced its contents, Chanda's charity was all he had.

Roberta turned and shook her head. "Put that away, kid. This one's on me."

He thanked her.

Back at the outdoor table, Simón worked through his breakfast while Roberta sipped coffee and drummed her fingernails on the fiberglass.

"So, Simón," she started. "We've been friends for a week, and I barely know anything about you. Apart from your interest in birds and sinkholes, anyway."

Friends. Simón chewed and nodded, mulling it over. He supposed they might as well be. He'd spent more time with this stranger than almost anyone else in months. "There's not much to know."

"You're some kind of artist, right? Chanda said you're hella talented."

"Not really. I used to dabble, but not so much anymore."

"Oh, please. There's no hiding it, Simón. Your art

emanates from you. Plus, I saw that sick mic the other day."

"I mean, I went to grad school for experimental music."

"No shit? Well, consider my curiosity piqued," Roberta said. "You'll have to let me listen."

"And you?" Simón asked. "You're a..."

"Teacher," she said, rolling her eyes. "High school chemistry. I was supposed to be a quantum physicist, but my college advisor talked me out of it. That was the last time I let anyone tell me what to do with my life. Including my ex-wife!" She chuckled wistfully.

The food came quickly, and shortly thereafter, bore a hole through Simón's stomach lining. Roberta downed her King Dog, then delicately patted away the leftover cheese from the sides of her mouth.

"You wanna get out of here?" she asked. "I'll drive you home."

Scarlet maples bobbed over the patio tables, wearing the sky like a blurred silver jacket. Above their ancient dance, an osprey, mid-flight, screamed in agony.

The bird plummeted toward the tree canopies, faster and faster. Trailing behind it, a deflated balloon on a long string. Against the roar of wind, the osprey struggled against the dead balloon with hopeless fluttering wings, casting a dragonesque silhouette. It cried out a third, final time before vanishing behind the horizon.

The pain in its cry echoed through Simón's mind. He fantasized about slowing and diluting that bellow, its cries extended into an endless yearning drone. On and on.

Roberta asked for his address, green eyes reflecting her phone screen. She plugged it in her map, then turned to him. "You know, I'm an artist myself."

He shook himself loose from the bird's demise. "Yeah? Music?"

She nodded proudly.

"What kind?"

"It's— well, like I said, you never want to 'bias the results.' You dabble in, what, ambient-experimental?"

He nodded.

"Well, *hopefully* that means you also dig…" she lowered her voice an octave, imitating a radio show host, "— braindance with a mix of Nordic pastoral-ambient and doomgaze." She watched his face, perhaps waiting for a look of recognition that never came. "Here, it's easier just to play it."

She plugged in an aux cord, queued up a track, and let it rip. The blend of genres was unlike anything Simón had ever heard.

"This is seriously phenomenal, Roberta. What — wait, are those synths?"

"Oh, that's my washing machine. I just put a ton of delay on it."

"No kidding. And where did you find the vocal samples for the screaming?"

Roberta grinned mischievously. To Simón's complete surprise, she unleashed a searing, brutal black metal growl.

"No fucking way," Simón said.

"Hell yeeees!" she howled.

They laughed, listening to one song after another as she wove around slower cars. Roberta was a terrifying driver, making free use of the horn and her arsenal of expletives as she careened through traffic. Flutes, vibraphones, and sitars jangled as a steady bass thumped, guiding Simón deeper under a resplendent veil. A choir of reverbed screams emerged, penetrating the aural haze.

"It's my newest album," she said, lowering the volume a little. "I have five out right now, and this one's called *Stranger on the Seventh Floor, I Gave My Heart to You*. It's inspired by a tuxedo cat I was friendly with in my building," she sighed. "Rest in peace, Moe."

"Rest in peace, Moe," he repeated.

Listening to her music, how whole and encompassing it was, Simón revisited the falling osprey and its ailing cry. He wished he'd recorded it. That was a missed opportunity. Its descent felt personal; he longed to contain it, to bring it home, to preserve its pain. If he could add delay and parse out its sorrow, reorder the notes into something warmer, something languid and soothing, perhaps another message would've been waiting for him. But it was no use concerning himself now. The bird was gone, probably dead.

Roberta pulled up to his building. He thanked her for the ride, and she invited him to an upcoming performance. It'd be a small show, and she was only opening, but she'd appreciate his attendance.

"And, hey," she said. "Don't give up on those

recordings. I don't mean to get preachy, but I believe in a certain multidimensionality to things. Something is off-balance. Something needs unlocking and you've got the key, Simón. Call me when there's more. Maybe I can help."

❧

Chanda's bus money earned Simón a few days of sustenance in the form of frozen dinners and boxed soup. The kind of meal he could make with his eyes closed and head empty. He slowly worked his way through the little orange pill bottle on the counter, a prescription for Katrina Walsh, whoever that was.

Time passed, marked only by shadows crossing the walls. Lashes of thunder attempted to dislodge him from reverie, but the flagellation only soothed him. The tumultuous sky bulged with dark, arching clouds. A cloud bridge. But where did it lead? Out of this psychic fog?

Maybe Roberta was right. There was another dimension, one that contained or reflected his own, and its balance had been disrupted. Maybe the real world is the world of dreams, he thought. Or maybe she was crazy.

He sparked and puffed again from the bowl, letting the last of his stash restore him. His eyes glowed with unwept tears.

Then, he was outside his building; he didn't know why. At the sinkhole, he knelt by his recording equipment, the wind pushing his overgrown hair from his eyes. Then, he was inside again.

His phone rang again and again. First, Chanda, then Ma. Voicemails accumulated, threatening to puncture his protective shell. The real world was burdensome. Instead, he withdrew into dreams of resuscitating the dead osprey, of finding the unseen bird who'd spoken to him.

A half-sleep enveloped him. Great winds swept him into their embrace, and he drifted, drifted, drifted even further away.

Fledgling

A new cacophony. Shattering glass, or the wash of cymbals; pounding drums, or a stampede; the furious blare of car alarms or his neighbors slamming their doors in the hallway. He lay on the couch, fully clothed. His throat, parched, head throbbing.

Near enough to the balcony's sliding doors, he rolled over and pried open brittle eyelids. Hailstones the size of tennis balls pummeled Saint Pluvia. Radiance hummed, suppressed by charcoal clouds, making it impossible to gauge the time. His phone lay out of reach beneath the coffee table. He inched off the couch until his fingertips brushed the screen and revealed the hour. Just before noon.

Simón dragged his body to the miraculously intact sliding glass doors. The balcony was strewn with shards of broken glass from the smashed solar lantern. Above, a ferocious sky swirled, spewing ice.

He took a deep breath, stretched, and slapped his cheeks. First things first: brush his teeth, have breakfast, shower, and pull himself together, mimicking someone more functional like Chanda.

He found a two-day-old voicemail from her, inviting him to dinner. She wanted to show him the pigeons. Multiple pigeons. She might have gotten a little carried away, she'd admitted. There was another unread text too, this one from Roberta reminding him about that night's show. He wondered if there had always been so much happening on weekday evenings in Saint Pluvia.

He called Chanda to RSVP and apologized for the delay. "I can bring wine."

"Aren't you broke?" She laughed.

"Extremely."

"Just bring yourself."

"Well, maybe I can take you and Terrance out to a show after. No cover."

"You know I'm still doing the walk-to-work challenge, right? I have to be up at like six so I can take care of the birds before I go to the office. Not everyone is funemployed, you know." There was a stiff silence, and then she apologized. "That was shitty, I know. I haven't been sleeping much."

"Me neither," said Simón. It was sort of true. Despite drifting in and out of lucidity, the last few days were hardly restorative.

Later, under the shower's hot stream, he vaguely remembered taking his recording equipment outside. Whether it'd been last night or the night before or if it were just a dream, he wasn't sure.

Wrapped in a mildewed towel, he queued up the most recent recording. The timestamp was 1:07 AM. His pulse quickened when he heard an owl hooting. He focused, expecting a message. None came. Then, a low rumble. Rock breaking and scattering. His own voice, garbled by the scuffing of his feet and heavy breathing, asking, "What the hell?" Then, abrupt silence.

The nearly blacked-out memory of visiting the sinkhole drifted back into frame. There was a muffled explosion, then a glimmer from the depths. The pinprick of yellow grew wider and brighter. And impossibly, a hand draped in shadow appeared, then vanished into darkness.

Now outside, the hail had given way to gentle rain, sun peeking through clouds.

Back at the sinkhole, sober and in full daylight, Simón hopped the fence and searched for any sign of the mysterious light. There was nothing but sloped darkness. The abyss's depth and breadth were equal parts alluring and discomforting. He flattened himself on the ground for safety, poking his head over the edge and extending his arm, phone in hand and flashlight on, over the maw. As if in slow motion, the phone slipped and spiraled down. A lost cause.

The rain picked up again, eliminating the slightest chance of the phone's survival.

Another failure, he thought for a second, before realizing how little he actually cared. A weight lifted. He shut his eyes, suddenly aware of his hangover, and basked in the whirr of rinsing rainwater outside.

The rest of Simón's afternoon lay empty. He had hours to kill before heading to Chanda's place, and no desire to kill them. He debated his options — reading, doing a few pushups, shaving — but ultimately decided to rest.

His eyelids, a theater: July afternoons of two decades ago were bright and warm on the screen, just a few fluffy clouds in the sky. Abi's silky singing voice and the strum of his acoustic guitar rang loud over the pool. Playing on the backyard deck, his canary yellow shirt unbuttoned down to his chest, the broad collar sharp and crisp. With his thick silver mustache, Abi's smile was full of life. Every guitar strum, every wink from behind his sunglasses, every high note delivered fireworks.

Simón blinked his eyes open, dipping back into the present. Though he'd always remembered Abi as a filmmaker above all else, Simón vaguely recalled learning that Abi had written some jingles for television advertisements in Ecuador between film projects. The way Abi had talked about it, eyes gleaming with nostalgia, he was a big star in Ecuador. That's why he moved around so much, he'd said. Simón also remembered the way Ma shook her head and left the room whenever Abi told these tales.

Simón shut his eyes again in an attempt to return, but the memories had already fallen apart. This timbre, the recollection of his grandfather's serenade, was all that remained unbroken. He held onto the tenor like a talisman in his heart, weighing its heft against the void of himself.

Another three dollars vanished into the bus farebox, leaving just $21. He promised himself he'd call the bank and the police department tomorrow, and maybe make a DMV appointment to replace his license. What else had been in the wallet, apart from an obscenely expired condom? A couple receipts, a little cash. He broke out in a cold sweat, remembering — the photo. He'd been carrying around a faded image of a smooth-faced Abi, beaming as he cradled baby Simón thirty years prior. A crease ran across the image where it'd been folded in half to fit. Surely Ma had a copy, or a similar photo, hidden away somewhere. He hoped he was right.

When Chanda's apartment door swung open, she all but leapt on him.

"I didn't think you'd show!" She squeezed him into a vice-like embrace. "We just gave up and started cooking for ourselves."

"Why am I not surprised?"

She ushered him inside, pointing to the shoe rack. He added his mud-spattered canvas sneakers to the collection and followed her to the kitchen, where Terrance was artfully stir-frying vegetables.

"Smells good in here," Simón said. It was complex — vegetal and smoky, but also dusty and sour.

"Like a damn chicken coop," Terrance scowled.

The pigeons, Simón remembered. *Right.*

"And garlic!" Chanda laughed, wrapping her arms around her boyfriend's rotund waist.

"Yeah, yeah, yeah."

"He's just mad because I've been paying a little too much attention to my wards lately. But I have room in my heart for you too, birdy."

Terrance grinned and bent to kiss her head. "Sorry, it's just hard to share you."

Simón's eye twitched at the saccharine display. It wasn't that he didn't like Terrance. He just had a well-meaning stepfatherly vibe that was off-putting. "I'm gonna go wash up."

Apart from the shower — and the smell — the bathroom was as he'd remembered it, bright orange walls and an eclectic smattering of vintage postcards in gold frames from Chanda's collection. In the narrow glass shower stall, a trio of birds snuggled in an oversized plastic dog bowl lined with pine straw. The shower floor was caked with dried bird shit and fuzzy tufts of feathers. They cooed, curious, as he flushed, scrubbed his hands, and left the room.

"You're lucky, she cleaned up for you," Terrance said, scooping a saucy pile of crispy tofu and mixed vegetables onto Simón's bowl of brown rice. "They usually have free reign of the whole bathroom."

Chanda playfully punched her boyfriend's shoulder. Simón couldn't help but wonder how playful it really was. "You're making me sound crazy!"

"It's not all bad. Chanda stays at my place way more often now that she has to."

"It's a total bachelor pad." She leaned toward Simón.

"You'd love it. He's got speakers the size of phone booths."

"Oh yeah? What are you into, genre-wise?"

"Not into music, honestly. I'm more of a home theater guy," Terrance said, mid-chew. "You should come over sometime. Me and the guys do Marvel marathons on Sundays."

Simón nodded politely, refusing to betray his repulsion toward comic book blockbusters.

"That's the real reason we don't live together." Chanda laughed.

"That and the pigeons," Terrance said.

"About that—" Simón interjected, jumping at the opportunity to change the subject. "How did you end up with three? Your voicemail—"

"So, you did listen to it."

"I did. I'm sorry—"

"I'm just fucking with you." Chanda grinned. "Okay, so you know about the first one."

"Picasso?"

"Right. So, I take Picasso to the vet so they could set his wing and patch up his beak, then I bring him home to settle in. I decided to work from home, so I can keep him comfortable. I'm sitting, working at this very table, when something slams into the window behind us." She smacked her palms against the table for emphasis, rattling the dishes. "Outside, there in the grass, is another fucking pigeon. I was like, well, shit, I'm already set up for it. I grabbed it, put out another few hundred bucks to bandage up his sorry ass, and added him to the aviary."

Terrance chuckled in spite of himself.

"So, that's two," Simón said.

She nodded. "Later that week, I have an in-person workday. I do my little commute and when I get to the office, nobody's in their cube. Everyone's gathered in the conference room. I get excited because usually that means bagels, and I've been out of breakfast groceries for days, what with this whole rescue operation. Guess what these motherfuckers had."

"Donuts?"

"Another goddamn pigeon. It's like a fucking omen at this point. Nobody knows how it got into the building, but it was missing both legs and part of its beak. It can barely eat. Like it came in here to die or something. I call up the vet and she tells me there's no way to help this bird enough to re-release it into the wild. That the only humane option is euthanasia." With that, Chanda paused, and Terrance set down his chopsticks to stroke her back. "I think about my baba and his birds and I just... I don't know. I feel like I have to do this. Nobody else will." She dabbed at her eyes with an embroidered cloth napkin. "Anyway, that's how I became the bird lady of Cricket Ave." She laughed, then sighed. "But enough about me. How's the job search?"

He bobbed his head noncommittally. "Not great."

"It's a tough market," Terrance offered, and Simón agreed, as though he'd been making a concerted effort. "I can keep an eye out for you if you like. It's not audio engineering but sometimes we get openings for projectionists at the theater."

"I'd like that." A lie. Simón wasn't sure why he humored the suggestion despite vociferously declining career help from anyone and everyone; his mother, Chanda, even his old mentor who'd reached out on a professional social media platform when Simón added an end date to his Innovore position.

The conversation flat-lined, replaced by the scraping of chopsticks against bowls.

"I've been hanging out with Roberta," Simón said, at last.

Chanda raised a finely groomed eyebrow.

"We went to Chili Dog Kingdom."

"Great spot," Terrance said. "Every order comes with a free side of heartburn."

"I didn't think you two would have much in common. She's kinda, you know... wacky."

"She's a musician too. Besides, I'm getting the sense that most bird-people are 'wacky,'" Simón said.

"Wait, birdwatching Roberta?" Terrance interjected.

Simón nodded, mouth full.

"Interesting," he said, breaking eye contact.

Simón figured she must've told him about Roberta. But what was there to tell? She was a friendly middle-aged chemistry teacher. More importantly, the only person who took him seriously. Besides, Simón's own life was far from normal. Who was he to judge?

"I think she's nice," he said. "She's the one who invited me out tonight, actually. You sure you don't wanna come? Show starts at eight."

Terrance and Chanda locked eyes in silent debate. He shrugged and she scowled.

"Like I already said, we're gonna stay in," Chanda said. "Thanks anyway."

He glanced at the wall clock. "I should probably leave soon. The show's northside of town."

"Please tell me you're not walking."

"Nah, I've still got the transfer from my trip over here. Thanks for the cash, by the way."

Terrance glared at Chanda.

"I paid him back for something else," she explained, before shooting Simón a dirty look. "I'll walk you out."

Before closing the door behind him, she whispered. "Sorry, you hit a tense topic. I borrowed some money from him to cover the vet bills and he's unhappy about the whole thing. It's whatever. We'll figure it out." And with that, she winked and slipped Simón a wrinkled twenty-dollar bill.

Willing to Forget

Simón felt like half of his brain was missing without a phone. Thankfully, the venue's address was memorable: *10 Tree Lobster Way.*

Off the bus, freezing rain swept him through the mouth of a wind tunnel, a narrow street between rowhomes. Drenched head-to-toe, he looked up at the sky for the golden moon, flashing with devilish, freeing promise.

It'd been days since he'd been this sober, and it felt good to be alive, to see multiple friends in a single day. *When was the last—* he stopped mid-thought to avoid drowning in the past.

Not a venue in sight, only homes. *Must be a private venue.*

He found the address and rang the bell. The door cracked open a few inches, the reckless laughter of guests spilling out. A lip-ringed face with sunglasses poked through the opening.

"I'm here to see—" he realized he didn't know Roberta's band's name. "Roberta's band. Uh— project."

"Name?"

"Oh. It's Simón."

The person raised their eyebrow high above their sunglasses, and Simón grew annoyed. He stuffed his hands into his pockets while the lip-ringed guard searched the guest list.

The interior was surprisingly spacious for a rowhome, especially with all the furniture cleared out. Among scattered groups of people, in the center of the wood-floored living room was a temporary stage with a microphone at the center, large speakers on either side.

It was the first time in months he'd squeezed through a crowd of thirty, forty people. Behind the stage, a large glass door led out to a patio. Hordes of guests crowded around the kitchen table, greedily ladling pink punch into plastic cups. A loud man shouted "Cheers!" in a faux-British accent.

He decided to wait outside until the line for the punch bowl died down. The rain had slowed to a fleeting patter. The backyard held beds of basil and rosemary, old pickle buckets brimming with fruitless tomato plants and mildewed vines of yellow squash. The rosemary had shriveled to a crisp, the basil drooped, and the squash vines sagged, limp and barren. Pink-spotted beetles meandered over every inch of it, feasting.

Out the kitchen door to the patio, a short butch-femme couple and their tall, ethereally beautiful friend stepped outside to smoke. The butch pulled an engraved silver lighter from the pocket of her denim jacket and held it to the femme's long cigarette. Their friend sucked on the tip of their blocky vape. Their conversation turned to a recent experimental dance album— "not enough piano," the femme said. "Too much piano," their tall friend countered, exhaling an herbaceous plume that drifted and enveloped

Simón. He listened carefully for a familiar artist's name, hoping to insert himself, but an opportunity never materialized. It was as if he'd lost all scene credibility in the years since leaving school.

He must have been staring. The couple glared at him while their friend chattered on, oblivious. "What, never seen queers before?" the femme spat, teeth bared.

Simón recoiled.

"Easy now," the butch chuckled, resting a hand on her date's thigh.

"I'm a friend of Roberta's," he said. "A new friend, anyway. She invited me. And I'm... you know."

The couple's faces softened. The tall friend's dark eyes tunneled into him. "Hey, wait, you're Mr. Field Recordings, right?" the friend asked. "The birdsong guy?"

"How do you...who told you—"

More people filtered out onto the patio, noticing the rain had slowed.

"The queen told us all about your project," the butch said.

"Blasphemous Simulation of Love herself," the femme said, starstruck.

He looked from face to face to face, searching for an explanation.

"Roberta." The femme rolled her dark-lined eyes.

"First time?" the butch asked.

He nodded.

"You're in for a treat. She's so good. Just a heads up,

these things get a little rowdy, at least for an IDM show. So, birdsong dude—"

"Simón," he said, receiving a curious look from the white couple. Compelled to explain the accent in his name, he added: "I'm half-Hispanic."

Because he'd never learned how to speak his mother's language, and because his skin was pale like his father's, all his life he carried the accent as a banner of selfhood. He'd always felt, growing up in a primarily white neighborhood, that there was little left of his heritage, even less with Abi absent, and whatever remained must be claimed outright. If Simón had known what an ordeal it'd be to get people to say his name correctly, if he'd known the harassment it'd provoke from racist strangers and xenophobic neighbors, then perhaps he would have given up in childhood, allowing himself to be perpetually renamed. But he'd recommitted to the fight after losing his job and refused to change course now.

"You don't look Mexican," the femme said.

"Well, because I'm not." He couldn't help laughing. "I'm Ecuadorian."

She blinked, unimpressed.

"I'd love to hear about your album," the butch said, perhaps to diffuse the tension.

The tall friend nodded in agreement, harboring a curious smile.

"It's not—" he struggled for the right words as the crowd outside grew. It soon felt cramped. A man with a massive backpack bumped into Simón from behind, sloshing punch onto the patio. Without thinking, Simón apologized and stepped aside from the puddle. "Yeah. It's not an album. It's more than that. I'm just using the sound to, uh, figure something out, you know?"

The femme stared blankly. The talkative crowd surrounding them filled the space, and he was yelling to compensate.

"Like I'm following something in the recordings."

Bored with the conversation, the couple started making out.

The tall friend finally spoke up. "Sounds like it's worth digging into. I'm Nausi, by the way."

"Mossy?"

"Nausi. Ever seen the Miyazaki film? *Nausicaä of the Valley of the Wind.*"

"Oh yeah." Simón's eyes widened. "That one's an all-timer. So, how do you know, uh, 'Blasphemy Sensation'?"

"Blasphe*mous* Simulation. Came across her stuff in art school. Pretty much all I learned there was how to stop enjoying normal-people music. Roberta's music was like a gateway for me. I don't usually go to her shows, but my friends insisted on taking me out. Plus, the venue's special. It's the guy from Helvetica Approach's old house."

"Helvetica?"

"Roberta's the opener tonight, Helvetica Approach is the main act. They always play together. Total psychonauts."

Simón nodded, feeling out of the loop.

Inside, the lights flickered, alerting everyone the concert was about to start.

"Good meeting you, Nausi," he said, before pushing through the crowd to the drink table inside.

Clenching his fists, Simón stepped to the punch bowl and poured a tall cup. He gulped, then refilled what he'd just drunk.

Why did Roberta tell people about the birdsong? he thought, waiting for the show to begin. *Does she think it's just a music thing?*

Supersaturated blooms of fog slithered upward from the audience's ankles. Lights from the stage's edge beaconed into the haze, painting the room alien-green.

Roberta entered from the back, waving. The crowd cheered. She stood by a stand with a laptop and keyboard, adjusted her mic, and scanned the audience. She pointed at him and leaned into the mic. In the barest whisper, she chanted his name. *Si-món. Si-món. Si-món.*

Simón tucked his shy grin inside the cup, sipping.

A woman sat down at the drums, and a man picked up a guitar, scooting the pedals closer to his feet. The crowd hushed, waiting.

A silence, a long, beautiful silence, where only the gentle droplets outside could be heard. The overhead lights darkened, and the stage glowed.

No longer a living room, but a chrysalis.

As the rhythm surged, a fever conquered his lungs, with breathing so sweet. The sparse silver rain still cascaded outside, and inside, the soul's oceans brimmed waterfalls, spores constellating at splash. Chartreuse tides accumulated beneath skin, through veins — his forearms, his legs — each time-stretched loop rewiring nerves and synapses. On some primal level, he could feel infancy's race toward the sparkle after death. Life, just a tunnel across a century. He swayed as a resynthesized wavelet, a buoy to a mellotron echo.

Afloat.

Were those his feet, or reeds of the Echo Bend ponds? His veins, or hallways of New Harbor's dorms? His eyes, or the Innovore skyscraper windows?

Calm to his core, Simón knew this wasn't from the alcohol.

While the drummer and guitarist maintained a rhythm, Roberta walked from her own guitar to the keyboard, adding layers to the rich texture, foot forever returning to the looper pedal. Finally, she found a place by her laptop to add decay and vocoder effects, and — despite Simón not thinking it possible — more echo. The drums picked up. Then, finally, she clutched the mic and unleashed a bouquet of screams.

Neither world nor machine. Forgot our one-body. I know love's tryptamine. Now I watch the stilled boats over frozen blood. Watch the void undone. I am no god, just dust, just winter. No light through stone, no window. Watch the void undone. I want to be undone.

He'd become a lantern, his skull's flats, curves, and sockets illumined bright, translucent. Green lightning eased into his bones, warm, fluxing, shimmering like piano trills.

Simón gazed at the lulling heads, faces obscured by vapor, spellbound by a blasphemous simulation of love. At the center of the head-nodders, a group of rowdy middle-aged fans formed a mosh pit, catapulting off each other. He laughed. He laughed again.

A pulsing bass-drum broke through the autumnal sheen, splitting the room into petals. Simón approached the speakers, careful not to spill his drink as he combed through the crowd. He closed his eyes, inviting sensation, reassurance to wash over him.

Nothing here can hurt you. The words, a truce.

There arose a peculiar but honest desire to reach out to Ma. *Maybe I'll text her to apologize. I could tell her I love her. I could tell her I forgive her, and I'm willing to forget everything.* His hand reached into his pocket but came up empty. *Oh well,* he thought.

Within moments, he'd forgotten the impulse to reconcile, buried in the blanket of sound. The pulse continued.

By the front door, Nausi ebbed and flowed between swaying shoulders, long hair trickling down from a messy bun.

Then, behind him, a crash.

A series of gasps followed, causing everyone to turn back toward the wide-open patio doors. The instruments stilled, the looping silenced. Simón's heart clanged in his chest.

A fawn, roughly the size of a large dog, had knocked over a tall lamp. White spots scaled its raised back as it took shelter beneath the kitchen table. Silent terror racked its jaw open, revealing a quartet of little teeth. A broken whimper, then loud, panicked bleating.

The crowd murmured. "Is it a possum or a baby deer?" someone asked from the sidelines.

Several others answered in unison. "A deer."

"Obviously," added another.

Simón saw Roberta onstage, and she nodded in silent affirmation. He crept toward the deer. It'd come for him.

Roberta's words echoed through his skull: *You've got the key.*

The fawn cowered as he squatted down beside the table, laying his hand upon it. Vicarious sadness coursed through him, flooding him with unlived memories of the deer's first months.

Music throbbed, not from the speakers, but from every atom of his goosebumped body, which seemed to extend beyond corporeal boundaries, coalescing, becoming, like the seafoam collecting on the sand.

Its short fur was coarse beneath his hand, yet softer than clouds. It peered through Simón, its dark, shiny pupils crowned in gold like turning leaves.

Simón answered, nodding. *Thank you, thank you.*

Tears streamed down his face, catalyzed by the vulnerable creature, and sustained by the new grace he bestowed upon himself.

It was only right that the animal stayed close, not fawning, but carrying out a task inscribed in its genetic codex, a whimpering key cloaked in fur the color of toasted wheat, smelling of moss and milk.

Fingertips on the back of his neck sent a rippling rush across his skin. He turned, slowly, remembering for the first time in seconds, or centuries, the house, the people, the stage.

The person leaning in from the emerald ambiance was familiar: the butch from before. A crowd pressed in behind her, their faces fading together.

She laughed, pupils dilated, and ran her short fingernails through Simón's overgrown hair. He grasped the faded blue denim of her jacket between his fingers. Again, he was a toddler in Abi's arms. He could smell the stale tobacco on the old man's jacket.

"She trusts you," the butch said.

"We trust each other," he said. "She's hurt."

The fawn, taking a few timid steps back and forth on the beige tile floor.

"What do we do now?"

"She knows what she needs," he said. "She's got the key. She is the key."

Simón caught Roberta's eye and nodded.

Cymbals rolled, washed, crashed, and the bass started up again. Either she was improvising, or she had orchestrated everything perfectly. No longer screaming, Roberta held a megaphone between her lips and the microphone. Her whispers swam in heavy synthesizer and rippled with delay.

"To fawn," she repeated along a steady beat.

The crowd joined in, carrying on the chant as Roberta growled a new verse on top of it.

"To crouch, to wait, to ride, to run, to spend, to give, to want, to be undone."

To be undone.

To be undone.

To be undone.

By the fourth refrain, he'd joined the chorus, mouthing along with Roberta's words, encouraging, or perhaps worshiping, the animal.

The fawn turned, dashed out through the patio door into the brisk night. The crowd parted as Simón took off in pursuit.

The small backyard gave way to dense trees, the firebrick glitter of maples and oaks in twilight. Fast under the moon, Simón listened for the delicate crinkle of snapping branches that marked the fawn's path. Now and again, he caught glimpses of the puffy tail ahead, outpacing him into the thicket.

Crisp air inflated Simón's lungs. His chest pounded.

Sweat gleamed and ran over his lips and into his mouth. An invisible tether trailed behind the fawn, pulling him from Saint Pluvia's northern outskirts into another world entirely. And then, just as quickly as it'd appeared, the forest ended.

He stopped under a buzzing streetlight at the edge of a quiet residential neighborhood. The fawn was nowhere to be seen. He closed his eyes, cool wind kissing his sweat-soaked temples. Anonymous, weightless; Simón, but a reflection of the moon. He stalled in the winking yellow, still buoyant with faith. The thrum of Roberta's music persisted within. And beyond the bounds of self, another rhythm: nearby water.

The tone drew him to the end of the block and around the corner. He advanced slowly. There, a streetlight illuminated a small bridge and the deer's silhouette.

His heart drummed. *Undone.*

From across the bridge came a doe's throaty, panicked call, just like the ones in his field recordings. The fawn lifted its head, then ran toward the sound.

Simón watched in awe as the mother licked, mewed, and danced around her child. Then, they both disappeared, gone into a world off-limits.

Alone, he rested his elbows on the bridge's metal railing and listened to creek water trickle around the rocks below. He closed his eyes and absorbed every note, a trillion crystals strewn across the darkness. Wind undulated through trees on the creek, tidelike, the fawn's golden chest, his own steady breath — the lapping creek, reaching, retreating, reaching, retreating — the dusk and dawn, ephemeral and endless.

"Simón?"

Simón shook himself back into the moment.

"Hey!" the voice called again.

He turned to find Nausi waving, tightly enveloped in a puffy jacket. Their hair was tied up, exposing pink, well-defined cheekbones.

"Goddamn," they panted. "You're faster than I expected."

From where Nausi approached, the pear trees heaved, fuchsia and white flags taut to the wind. Backlit by streetlamps, their enormous shadows draped like lace across the asphalt. The leaves' movement, flames on the pavement, eclipsed Nausi with their serpentine dance.

How the world reeked, damp like bourbon and decay. Every cricket rhapsodized about the divide of form from soul, about reincarnation, about the fathomless infinite. The streetlamp fizzled out as if defeated by moonglow.

Nausi found a spot beside him, leaning against the railing. Water sparkled over fallen leaves, littered cans, and the quartzite beneath. He peered at Nausi's profile, their heavy eyelids, and parted lips. They blew an herbal cloud, then held out the vape to Simón.

"Actually, I'm good, thanks. I feel *really* weird."

"I'm not so surprised," Nausi said. "At least half the party looked like they were on another planet."

"Yeah…" Simón tried to make sense of it, but it was like organizing a lava lamp's swirling goop. "I only drank two cups of punch. How many did you have?"

"I don't drink," they said, taking another hit. "I don't like feeling out of control."

"I kinda like it, honestly."

"Maybe that's worth examining. When you're not tripping."

"Tripping," he repeated, trying to parse out the meaning.

"Christ, you *are* high. I'm saying Roberta spiked the punch."

"The punch…" The lava lamp in his head snapped into orderly shapes. Roberta. Chemistry teacher. "The punch!" He burst out laughing.

Nausi started laughing too.

"Wait, what's so funny?" Simón huffed, trying to catch his breath.

"I just like the sound of your laugh," they said. "Also, I'm stoned."

Simón cracked up again. "You're nice."

"I am." They caught his eye for a fleeting second, then looked back out over the warbling creek.

"I'm thirsty."

"I live close by if you're interested. Maybe five minutes from here." They pointed into the dark distance. He contemplated this for a moment — his own apartment was miles away and wasn't sure how he'd find the right bus stop.

After a short, chilly walk, the pair approached a large suburban home on a sprawling, leaf-dappled lawn. There was a rented dumpster in the driveway, piled high with dirt and debris.

Simón fixated on his cotton mouth as he followed Nausi through the front door. In the kitchen, Simón gulped down two full glasses of water before Nausi tenderly placed a hand on his arm, encouraging him to pace himself. Thirst-tamed, he began to take in his surroundings. Pale oak cabinets with dingy brass knobs, off-white tile with gray grout, a wooden table with a vase of dusty, silk flowers perched in the middle.

"I like your house." He didn't but thought it would be rude not to acknowledge their decorating style.

"It was my parents'," Nausi said, setting a rusting kettle on the grease-spattered stove. The spout was missing its whistle, and the lumpy plastic handle looked like it'd melted and resolidified at some point. "I inherited it after they died."

"I'm sorry," he said, touching his chest. For all his angst, he couldn't fathom losing Ma. Losing Abi was hard, sure, but by the time his grandfather had died he'd been out of Simón's life for years.

"You didn't kill them. A semi-truck did." They shrugged as if it was just some banal, unremarkable anecdote and went to the corner cabinet to retrieve mugs.

He wasn't sure whether to laugh or apologize again. Instead, he focused on the strong muscles of their upper back and shoulders. Their pale skin was smooth, unmarked by ink, scars, or freckles.

"So, you grew up here?"

They nodded, placing herbal tea bags into each cup. "My uncle wanted me to sell it, but I didn't want to. You know how some people won't travel abroad until they've seen every state? That's how I feel about being here."

"Yes." Simón understood alright, more than he could ever express. He wanted to tell Nausi about the recordings, the infinite depth of his unfinished graduate work, the Butterfly sinkhole, but the words weren't coming. Instead, he reached out and clasped their warm hand between his own. "Yes," he repeated.

Nausi blushed.

Steam billowed from the kettle. Nausi filled the mugs, tinging the air with soothing lemon balm, then led him back into the living room. The worn, overfilled sectional swaddled them. It made perfect sense that Nausi would stay in this twentieth-century time capsule. What it lacked in aesthetic beauty, it made up for in comfort. The nostalgia was contagious, and Simón felt more at home than he ever had in his own stark apartment. It didn't look like his childhood home exactly — too colorless and generic without his mother's eccentric decor — but the textures were similar.

He glanced over at the side table, which held dust-caked family photos of a bland, but pleasant looking couple and their glittery-eyed son.

"You look different," he said, immediately regretting the words.

"Well, I'm a lot older now."

"And prettier."

"I am."

"Sorry, I shouldn't have said that." He glanced at the door.

"You seem anxious," Nausi said, readjusting the thin strap of their lace-lined camisole. They rose and went to the vintage stereo system, then tapped a couple buttons on the CD player. "This should help."

Brian Eno's *Music for Airports* trickled out from the bookshelf speakers, the familiar lullaby rippling through him, drawing out the dwindling psychoactive effects of the spiked punch to soothe his reawakening nerves.

Nausi placed a palm against his stubbled cheek, slowly tracing the shape of his jaw, the new wrinkles between his eyebrows, the dimples framing his mouth. "Is this okay?" they asked.

Simón nodded. Nausi smelled of mint and lavender, dark hair slipping back out of its bun and into their face. Their bright eyes overflowed with open curiosity. Their kiss was so soft he barely felt it.

"Do you want to go upstairs?" Nausi asked.

"I do. A lot. But I don't want you to feel obligated."

"Obligated?"

"To let me stay over."

"You're not planning anything weird are you?"

"Nothing weirder than what's already happened."

Nausi grinned. "Fair point."

And with that, they fell into each other, plummeting through the dark lush of desire.

Fucking Biblical

He woke alone, far more hungover than usual. Details of the previous night resurfaced, Chanda's pigeons, the punch, the fawn. Nausi. The bedroom, illuminated by the eastern-facing window, was small, carpeted like the rest of the house and peaked sharply in the middle. Band posters (Sufjan Stevens, Aphex Twin, Explosions in the Sky) plastered the angled walls, a stack of *Nintendo Power* magazines and *The Complete Works of William Shakespeare* beside a dusty albeit intricate Lego Bionicle Titan perched on the low bookshelf.

Yikes. The old posters didn't bother him, but the leftover detritus of childhood was uncanny, a little too reminiscent of his own former bedroom.

He extracted himself from the bed, careful not to smack his head on the low part of the ceiling. He wandered down the hallway looking for a bathroom, which was opposite an eerie main bedroom. The room was spacious and pristine with matching, oversized cherrywood dressers and a four-poster bed. The burgundy bedspread was striped to match the heavy curtains, piled high with decorative pillows and a large black-eyed teddy bear. He didn't know why he'd expected Nausi to have adopted their dead parents' bedroom but was ultimately glad they'd had sex in an intimate little nook instead of this plush, lonesome shrine.

He found Nausi in the kitchen making coffee.

"Caffeine?" they asked. "How are you feeling?"

"Not great," he said. "Not because of you, just because, you know."

"The surprise drugging?"

"Right. About that."

"Yeah, she's gotta stop doing that." Nausi rolled their eyes.

"I take it this isn't the first time?"

They nodded, sipping. "Most people know what to expect from her shows by now, but every now and then someone has to find out the hard way. It's a rite of passage among her diehard fans. My friends say she used to just play her sets and keep her chemistry experiments to herself. I'm not sure what changed."

He scrounged around for empathy. Maybe her divorce had pushed her even further outside the bounds of socially accepted behavior. It'd happened to him, in a way — one minute he was fighting climate change with one of the region's largest employers, the next he was going on benders and playing near sinkholes.

"Isn't she worried someone will call the cops on her?" he asked. "I can't imagine everyone's down for unplanned trips."

"It's a very well-vetted invite list, mostly diehard fans. Plus, she's pretty secretive about her real identity."

"You knew about it."

"I used to be her student, way back when."

"Wait, how old is she? And—" he did his best to not

sound awkward, "how old are you?"

"She's upwards of forty, I think. I'm twenty-six."

Simón nodded, relieved. He'd hoped Nausi would be his age, but twenty-six wasn't bad. He wondered how old they'd been when their parents died — the house felt like a portal to the early 2000's at the latest. Had they been here alone since then? If so, who had raised them?

"I'm thirty."

"You're old."

"To a twenty-six-year-old."

"I was joking," they clarified.

"Right." The acidic coffee audibly churned his stomach. "I don't mean to impose—"

Outside his apartment, Simón lingered on the car door handle. He debated whether to give Nausi a kiss before leaving. He still hadn't processed his emotions from last night. Before he could make up his mind, Nausi leaned across and planted a quick kiss on his cheek.

"Call me sometime?" Nausi fidgeted with their sunglasses.

"My phone's at the bottom of a sinkhole," Simón said, straight-faced.

They laughed. "Then maybe, like, send me a messenger pigeon?"

"Believe it or not, that might be an option."

Climbing the stairs to the third floor was a struggle. His brain clicked and banged against the inside of his skull, and his hamstrings burned from running through the neighborhoods. Back in the sterile, new-construction apartment building, all of it felt like a dream.

In this quasi-conscious state, he almost missed the sheet of paper taped to his door. "FINAL EVICTION NOTICE" shouted out in bold red font, followed by small, blurry print. When had he received his first eviction notice? He tore the paper from the door and skimmed the details. He had ten days to vacate.

Plenty of time.

His own nonchalance shocked him. This was serious, he knew. And yet, something about it felt inevitable.

The neighbor from across the hall, a well-heeled Czech man carrying an armful of dry-cleaned suits, glanced away as Simón exited the apartment as if to avoid acknowledging what he'd seen on his door. It hadn't occurred to Simón that he should be embarrassed, although this would have been mortifying and unimaginable a few months ago. He tried to sort out when he'd last paid rent but couldn't recall.

Bereft of answers, Simón flipped through some of his prized "escapism" records: *Rhythm of the Saints, Heart of the Congos, Spirit of Eden, Novus Magnificat, Deloused in the Comatorium, The Pavilion of Dreams, Dream Theory in Malaya, Oil of Every Pearl's Un-Insides, Acid Mt. Fuji,* the *Twin Peaks* score... Instead, he queued up the album Nausi had played the night prior.

He decided against showering, perhaps to hold onto their touch a little longer. Even in its cluttered, lived-in state, the apartment felt desolate. It was strange; he'd gotten used to being alone for days, weeks on end, but after a single night away, he longed for Nausi's quiet comfort. He ached to tell them everything.

The urge to share, even stranger than this new craving for nearness. He'd initially been mortified when those people at Roberta's show asked about his "album," furious at Roberta both for gossiping about him and getting the facts wrong. But in the light of day, the exchange had made him feel like a real artist again. Even if only a handful of people knew him as a musician, which meant something, confirmed there was something special about him.

Recording the birdsong was mere instinct; it was relaxing to edit ambient sounds. But what he found inside them was— he didn't even know what to call it. Messages, hallucinations, the voice of a demon? Whatever it was, it probably just confirmed he was losing his mind.

An album, he pondered. A long-dormant urge to create awakened within.

He opened the editing software, then gathered and layered all of the birdsong recordings from the past few days. No matter how he arranged it, it never became discordant. It always sounded just right. Then, he dug into the obscure corners of sample libraries, searching, extracting, diluting, delaying, overlapping — a chemistry project in itself. Surrounded by limitless possibilities of sound, Simón's face warmed. Eventually, he realized several hours had passed since first sitting down. The track now exceeded ten minutes. Listening back to it, he wasn't exactly impressed, but there were moments of potential.

A notification popped up in the corner of his screen. An email from his aunt. He wanted badly to just ignore it, just as he had his mother's attempts to reach him. He finally felt at peace with his phone gone. He didn't need people hounding him with messages and demands he didn't have the energy to process. But an email from an estranged relative was unusual enough to worry him.

A freewheeling artist he barely knew, Tía Cecilia had never bothered to reestablish contact with him post-adolescence. Why reach out now unless someone had died? He braced himself for bad news.

His unread messages were in the tens of thousands. Mostly junk. The email from Cecilia, with no subject line, was the most recent. Another jumped out: an email from Chanda earlier that morning. He opened his aunt's first.

Simón,

Your mom tells me you're not answering your phone? She's super worried. I mean, she'd have to be to loop me in. Give one of us a call or email, will you?

Ciao,
Cecilia

P.S. I've attached a photo of me from my last residency in Italia! I know it looks like gray hair, but it's just flecks of paint. Your mom says you're an artist too — would love to see your work.

In the photo, a happier, wild-haired version of his mother leaned against a worn stone archway. She wore yellow clogs and white ripped-up overalls, both freckled with paint. It was like peering into an alternate universe, one he wished he'd been privy to all along. Simón began drafting a response but stopped. He promised himself he'd answer later, send some old music or his new work-in-progress, or at least summon the will to call once he'd replaced his phone. Next, he opened Chanda's email.

Your phone's still going straight to voicemail, so I guess you haven't dived down into the mouth of hell to get it back. If by some miracle you're checking your email, get back to me ASAP. I'm taking an extra long lunch break, and I could use your help with something. I'll even buy you a slice of pizza, Mr. Starving Artist. I have this new project. Maybe it would do you good to give back.

Simón filled in what he assumed was the implied ending of the final sentence:

Maybe it would do you good to give back all the help I've given you instead of just thinking about yourself.

He resented that she would even imply it. Didn't she understand what he was going through?

Still, free pizza was tempting. He shot back an email, leaving out the bitterness:

Let's do it.

❧

Simón got off at the bus stop half a block from Chanda's office. It was a small space on the ground floor between a shoe store and a real estate office. Posters advertising community food drives and after school programs plastered the window.

Chanda stepped out lugging an oversized camping backpack bursting at the zippers.

"You hungry?" she asked.

"Very. What's in the bag?"

"I'll show you in a sec. Keep up," she said, winding through stalled traffic.

Outside the pizza place, Simón stuffed his face as Chanda pulled one of a dozen-plus manila envelopes from her bag. She showed Simón the contents: a stack of stickers and an explanatory brochure. The stickers were black silhouettes of hawks that could be stuck on windows to prevent birds from crashing into them.

"We have to fix this problem at the roots, you know?" Chanda said. "Dead birds everywhere. It's fucking biblical."

"So, you want me to..."

"Bring these to office buildings, especially the tall ones

with lots of glass. We could split up and cover more ground."

Simón stared at her blankly.

Chanda sighed. "Or we can go together, whatever."

"Sorry, I'm just a little off today."

She raised her eyebrows as if to say what else was new, then plowed ahead, Simón skipping to keep up.

"I take it you had fun last night?"

"It was… interesting."

"Interesting good or interesting bad?"

"A little of both. Mostly good. I, uh, went home with someone."

"That is interesting!" Chanda seemed pleasantly surprised. "Who's the lucky lady?"

"Well, uh…"

"Or fella?"

"Uhhh…"

"Got it. Did you pick them up at the concert?"

"They kinda picked me up."

She elbowed him gently. "Good for you! I don't have to tell you how long it's been."

He didn't need the reminder; it'd been at least six months since his last hookup, that sweet but dull coworker from customer experience. And prior to her was a brief, torrid affair with a closeted married man and coke addict who compulsively made false promises. That was it. His dry spell wasn't for lack of opportunity; it was just that work had taken priority over everything.

They pushed through a revolving door and into a cavernous marble lobby surrounded by security guards. At the center, a bored-looking receptionist with an exacting bowl cut asked who they were here to see.

"The facilities manager," Chanda announced.

"You need to make an appointment."

"I just wanted to offer you these anti-collision window decals. They're from the Audubon Society."

"I'm not at liberty to purchase things on behalf of the company."

"No, no they're free," Chanda pressed on.

"I can't accept gifts either."

"But they keep birds from smacking into the windows!" Chanda's foot tapped impatiently. She looked to Simón for help, but he wasn't sure how to fix the situation.

"We don't have a bird problem."

"You absolutely have a bird problem. I've been scraping them up off your fucking sidewalks all week."

"Ma'am, there's no reason to use that kind of language. Please, calm down."

"Calm down?! This is a matter of life and death!"

Overhearing the escalation, the guards started walking toward them.

"So that's how it's gonna be." Chanda turned back to the door. "I'll see myself out. Come on." She grabbed Simón's sleeve and tugged.

Back outside, Chanda ripped open an envelope and peeled a decal off its backing, then smacked it against the pane of glass.

"You're fucking welcome!" she screamed, staring down the receptionist through the window.

She bolted, Simón struggling to keep up. They caught their breath in a nearby alley.

"Can you believe that bullshit?" Chanda huffed. "God, what ever happened to empathy!"

Hands on his knees, Simón wheezed, unable to answer, then gagged, spitting strings of drool onto the sidewalk.

"Jesus, how much did you drink last night?"

"Just two cups."

"Of Everclear?"

"Punch."

"And then what, no sleep?"

"I slept."

"Then why are you so wrecked, dude?"

He sighed and lowered himself to the sidewalk, resting his head against the brick wall. "Ecstasy. Or something like that, it's hard to say."

"Not this again," she said, squatting down to meet his gaze. "I feel like we just got you back down to normal drugs."

He looked down at the alleyway's cracked cement, remembering Katrina Walsh's dwindling bottle of Xanax on the kitchen counter.

"It wasn't on purpose."

"So, what, your date drugged you?"

"No, god no. Someone spiked the punch."

"Oh, Simón! That's horrible! Did they get everyone?"

"Not my, uh, not the person I went home with. Nausi. They don't drink. But I think they got almost everyone else. Nausi says Roberta did it."

"Did what?"

"Spiked the punch."

She was disgusted. "Why would she do that?"

"I don't know. Maybe for the vibe or something. It goes well with her act — did you know it's called Blasphemous Simulation of Love? Crazy." He laughed, shaking his head.

"It's not funny, Simón. She could have killed someone."

"What? Nobody died."

"How would you know? Were you even there the whole time?"

"No, I left; but her fans—"

"I feel like you're missing the entire point!" She leapt up and paced from one end of the alley to the next, righteous fury reignited. "What the hell, Simón. I don't wanna blame you for getting drugged but, like, you've lost all perspective. I feel like you're spiraling out of control. Again."

Simón was unbearably thirsty. The water bottle in the pouch of Chanda's backpack sloshed.

"Do you think I could get a sip?" Simón asked, pointing to it.

"Are you even listening to me?"

Simón slid down the graffiti-covered wall and sat on the dirty asphalt. Chanda reached for her water bottle and dropped it on his lap.

"Yeah, I'm listening. I've lost all perspective, I'm spiraling, I'm a drug-addled failure. Am I missing anything?"

"I don't know," Chanda said, folding her arms at her chest. "Is there anything else you wanted to tell me?"

Simón took a gulp of water. "Well, I did get evicted today," he said. "Or maybe yesterday, I'm not sure."

Chanda stood speechless, aghast.

"Hey, I was going to ask: maybe after this, could you drop me at the DMV in South Millipede Plaza? There's a phone store and bank right there, too, I think. I could replace all my things in one go."

A car alarm went off several blocks away. Its growing anger filled the silence. *Alarms: manufactured with the intent of distress.* Each note he imagined was carefully selected to rouse the tired and to drive panic. *Now that's a miserable job. Siren composer.*

Her eyes closed and she slowly inhaled, then exhaled.

"Dude," she finally said, "I'm not your mother. It's fan-fucking-tastic you've decided to rejoin the real world. But it was like pulling teeth to get you moving again. Months without a word from you. I'm always calling, knocking, begging you to come for dinner. I've never judged you no matter what you pull. I gave you bus fare again and again, despite being broke as shit myself, not that you cared. You're too fucked up to notice that you're not the only one having a hard time. And it's been like this since college. I'm always *that* friend for you." She sighed. "And it's like, would it kill you to just once be that friend for me?"

"I'm sorry for being such a burden." Simón didn't know what else to say. He stood and brushed his palms on his pants.

She lifted her face to the narrow columns of sky between skyscrapers, surveying for travelers in-flight.

She sighed heavily. "I'm not calling you a burden."

The car alarm continued.

"So, about that ride..."

She scoffed. "Fine, sure. I won't be the reason you lose your apartment. But I'm just dropping you off," she said, nodding toward the building he leaned against. "Then, I'm coming back to make these fuckers sticky their goddamn windows."

Little to Simón's knowledge, the shopping center had changed over long ago. He hadn't been to the city center since leaving Innovore. The phone store and bank were no longer there, replaced by another Chili Dog Kingdom and shops selling faux marijuana vapes, impotence edibles, and expensive herbal supplements amassed from endangered plants.

As they pulled into the lot, Simón didn't have the heart to tell Chanda the phone store and bank were nowhere to be seen. He simply thanked her and wished her luck with her campaign for pigeon safety. As she drove, the sky darkened, and the heavens opened up.

It's always raining now.

After waiting in line for over an hour at the DMV, he was told to mail in an application. He asked for a temporary ID, but the clerk demanded he submit the paperwork from home, or magically produce two forms of proof of residence, a social security card, and a forty-dollar check. He left empty handed.

Outside, the rain heaved like ocean waves, slapping against parked cars. He stood under the shopping center's awning for a while, waiting for the storm to pass, then gave up and ducked into the vape store.

The door chimed as he entered, a bell signaling the start of meditation. A vapid sort of peace always awaited him in stores like this. The customers were his people, all seeking relief, all holding their pain so sacred.

Acid rose in his stomach, then esophagus.

Standing beside a cabinet full of different capsules, he read their descriptions: one for chronic pain, one for sexual lethargy, one to encourage talkativeness (particularly to strangers), one to unbury ancestral truths about oneself and one's own family; each borne of a different species of rare plant, or microscopic algae found in coral, or a vitamin found in a near-extinct mollusk's slime, or a symbiotic culture baptized in a laboratory to safeguard the human body.

If only he had money to spend on a single miraculous

medication, not that anything could solve his core issue — whatever it was. There had been a temporary cure at Roberta's show; he still felt the music soaring within, charging through his bloodstream, sublime. He'd uncovered a wonderful forgiveness for everyone and everything, including himself, but the feeling hadn't lasted, leaving a burning in its place.

He was tired of waiting. Rain clobbered down as he crossed the plaza. A handful of pedestrians bolted to their cars, or into stores, their inside-out umbrellas made useless by the wind. He thought he heard a fawn's bleating, but it was only the squeal of truck tires on wet pavement.

The clouds grew denser, casting premature night across Saint Pluvia. A mute fog hovered down Slug Avenue toward the Innovore skyscraper. Passing headlights dimmed, flattened by the impenetrable haze. Drivers set their hazard lights on, a futile gesture amid the blur.

Along the rest of the rain-rinsed skyline, the Millipede telecommunications tower pulsed in time with Innovore, and to the west, the torchlight of a petrochemical plant's steam cracker blazed, venomous. Abandoned cathedrals-turned-nightclubs, rowhome after rowhome after apartment building atop a grocery store atop a CrossFit gym; he scanned their windows, all dark and lifeless.

On the corner, the enormous Innovore building loomed, spires blading toward the invisible sun. Scarlet lights strobed beyond the gray blanket, gems in the tower's crown. Below, hawks haloed for the dead.

Tears streamed down his cheeks, mixing with rain. He'd convinced himself things were about to get better. What had he been thinking? He had no job, no phone, no wallet, no ID. And now, no home. Fate had abandoned him, just as he'd abandoned his family. Months of ignoring Ma had made Simón exactly like his father.

The chaos of the storm drew all the attention of passersby, huffing and puffing as they sought shelter and, at least for that, Simón was grateful. In the downpour, no one so much as tried to recognize him; gracious anonymity. He drifted, aimless.

The Innovore receptionist was distracted clearing out a massive puddle in the lobby. He tailed a long-bearded man through the turnstile. The man turned and waited for an explanation.

"I'm new and my boss has my badge," Simón said.

"So, wait in the lobby."

"Not what my new boss told me to do."

"Sounds like your boss is screwing up your first day. Red flag numero uno." The bearded man snorted. His breath smelled of alpine mint and cigarettes.

Simón looked away, to the nearby neglected ping-pong table in the cross-wing hallway. The glass huddle room on its right brimmed with people, each staring mute into their monitors.

"Don't worry about it, man. Enjoy the 'vore." He leaned forward and whispered. "Seriously the best pay you'll ever get, for doing next to nothing."

"What do you mean?"

"I'm working on an SOP for an SOP, man. I was hired as an instructional designer. I haven't designed anything. It's hilarious."

The organism was running as it always had on fumes of self-referential pretense. "That's great," he said flatly.

He made his way to the fair trade coffee station as though he'd never left. A cheerful, passive-aggressive sign encouraged employees to use the biodegradable cups sparingly, reminding them of the branded travel mugs they'd received in their welcome kit. The espresso was delicious, reflux be damned. The buzz came immediately, sharpening his vision. He hadn't realized how tired he was.

Edison, Carnegie, Bezos; the first floor's open working spaces were each named after different titans of industry. Table upon table of workers, lost in a field of screens. Continuing down the wing, he passed the triple auditorium, the in-office spa (never-to-be-used), the cafeteria, then another working space, identical to the one before it. Fully absorbed in their monitors, the workers didn't notice Simón, or the deluge that trailed behind him like a marker of his sorrow. His headache worsened under the fluorescent lights, nerves vibrating, stomach acid searing his esophagus.

The twentieth floor's glass-enclosed cloud bridge was uncharacteristically deserted. He'd spent so many mornings in step with the zombie-like procession of his colleagues, marching from one skyscraper to its sister.

Beyond the connector's glass panes, the storm enshrouded the city, making the bridge feel like a labyrinth buried in the earth, or a great elevated artery in the night.

The glass was cool, steamed by his warm breath. The peaks of shorter buildings slicing through the hovering fog, the petrochemical plant's torchlight danced a hypnotic red, red, red.

His steady gaze broke when a hawk swept, barely avoiding collision, lost in the pandemonium.

Entering the bridge across the way was none other than the founder himself. Ansel opened the double doors from the sister tech center. He walked with intent, donning a sleek tan turtleneck and snug, highwater tweed slacks, flanked by chattering sycophants in Innovore-branded fleece half-zips.

Ansel's cool, effortless expression fell away, replaced by disorientation. "Simon!"

"Ansel."

"What— how—" Ansel's eyes dipped to Simón's hands which rested, mercifully unarmed, at his sides. He paused and took a meditative breath, recomposing himself. "To what do I owe the pleasure?"

He hadn't planned this far ahead, assuming it'd be too difficult to bypass security. "I guess I was just... feeling nostalgic."

Ansel's face brightened, charmed. "Nostalgic!"

His colleagues — a former frat boy and a pair of nearly identical young women with taut ponytails and subtle makeup — each held Innovore mugs and tablets, not a single-use object in sight. Sustainability chic.

"Simon was one of our most brilliant contractors," Ansel told them. "Unfortunately, the project changed directions, but we'd love to bring him back home when budgets and priorities align."

Home. The word stung.

The sycophants smiled wanly, heads empty. A heavy pause hung in the air.

"Good to meet you, Simon!" one of the women finally said.

"It's Simón." He locked eyes with Ansel. As if possessed by despair, a question rose to the surface and spilled from his lips. "What was I building?"

"What are any of us building?" Ansel countered, chuckling to his cronies. "A better world. A better future. It's so easy to lose sight of that, with all the miniscule daily tasks that make up the work. But together—"

Simón cut him off. "No, Ansel. Not us. Me. What was I building?"

"You know we can't discuss that now. Security clearances," he scolded, all but wagging his finger. He turned to the others, apologetic. "No offense."

The trio shrugged, unbothered.

"I think I was building something bad."

Ansel, perhaps sensing Simón's tears, leaned over to whisper to one of the women. She excused herself and she scurried over the cloud bridge, back into the tech center without looking back.

"You don't have to do this," Simón said, unsure exactly what he meant. "I mean, you could do anything. You're already rich! You could be running marathons or exploring caves or sailing around the world. You have a choice. And what choice did I have? You told me I could join you or starve as an independent artist. But you lied. 'Cause I joined you, and I'm gonna starve anyway."

An elevator dinged in the near distance. A stampede of boots drummed toward them.

Simón had nothing left to say.

Ansel mumbled; speech too soft to register. It wasn't until the guards tossed Simón onto the hard cement outside that the man's words fell into place.

I'm sorry.

The Only Option

I t was nearly dark by the time he arrived at Earhart High, emotionally drained and soaking wet. Initially built to house a junior college, the campus was divided into concrete buildings by subject. He wove between structures, passing tagged lockers and overflowing trash cans, remembering the brutality of his own high school years. The merciless taunting, the ostracization, the indignity of being loathed for his precocity. The science building appeared before him, windows glowing with promise. Roberta peeked up from her cluttered desk, delighted to see him.

"Hey stranger!" She leapt up to hug him, then recoiled. "Did you fall into a fountain or something?"

He laughed in spite of his dour mood. "Hit a patch of bad weather."

"I haven't been outside in hours," she said, pointing to a massive stack of papers. "Midterms."

"Already?"

"I know. Snuck up on me too. Here—" She opened a desk drawer and pulled out a gym towel. "Just don't sniff it."

He patted himself dry, careful to avoid his face.

"Sit, sit."

Simón squeezed into one of the front row desks, knees rammed up against the writing surface.

"Don't tell me you've got a science question," Roberta said. "I've already gone over covalent bonds more times than I can count."

"I was just in the neighborhood," he lied. His feet ached from the mile-long walk uptown to the most historic part of the city, back near where he'd started that morning. "Also, I was hoping you might have Nausi's number."

"My Nausi?"

"Yeah, from the show."

"What for?"

"You know, uh, for hanging out."

"Didn't know you swung that way." She nodded approvingly. "I like you even better now."

"Thanks, I think?"

"I'll just text it to you." She reached for her purse.

"Actually, I still don't have a phone."

"Jesus, still? That would explain why you haven't acknowledged all the links I've been sending. It was good shit, too. Did you know birds can use quantum entanglement to see the earth's magnetic field? And now they're saying their songs have quantum elements too. Seemed right up your alley, figured you'd wanna know."

"I'm sorry," Simón said, echoing Ansel's words from earlier.

"Don't be, I figured you were busy. And now I know why." She winked lasciviously, then scribbled a couple phone numbers down on a slip of scrap paper. "That one's Nausi, this one's me. Just in case."

"Thanks. Mind if I get Chanda's too? I should have had it memorized by now, but you know how it is." Roberta nodded, then flicked through her phone and added it to the paper. She'd been so helpful he'd almost forgotten about the punch. "Hey, uh, one more thing."

"Mm?"

"About the show. I drank something and, uh…"

Her eyes sparkled with mischief and a sly grin crept across her magenta-tinted lips. "Blasphemous Simulation of Love knows not of what you speak." She glanced down at the piled papers. "I'm almost done grading. If you can wait a bit, I'll drive you home."

The ride back was a brief moment of terror due to Roberta's speeding. There was a brief respite from the rain. Flocked with jack-o-lantern clouds, the sky lapsed and resumed its tantrum.

"The way I see it, I'm helping people break through," Roberta said, now that they were a safe distance from her employer. "Everyone's so hung up on categorizing things. True, false, right, wrong, animal, mineral, gay, straight." She elbowed him. "Even I'm guilty of it. But life isn't so simple is it?"

Simón nodded. She was right. He was sick of the black and white dilemmas that had infested his art practice. Experimental, deluded. Good, bad. Finished, unfinished.

"Everyone thinks science provides a set of clear boundaries between things that are and things that are not. But if you're doing it right, science asks just as many questions as it answers. Like, how can quantum-level particles occupy multiple states at once? Or how can entangled particles communicate across great distances? It both is and isn't magic."

"What does that have to do with spiked punch?"

"Everything!" she shouted, slapping the steering wheel. "If we only ever use our minds in an unaltered state, we only see the world's surface level traits, a veneer of uncomplicated so-called *truths*. Haven't you ever wondered about our essence, the indivisible transparent realm that *refuses* to separate a whole into parts? The way I see it, if you can change the way you think, you can change the way you see. You can break through the wall."

❧

That evening, Simón sank into the back seat of a cab. He'd ordered it the old-fashioned way, waving down a passing taxi, luggage in tow. The driver warned it'd be expensive. But what choice did he have?

On Redundo Bridge, the metropolis faded behind him. Never-ending globs of rain punched the windows. Perhaps he should have waited out the storm, but there was a sense it'd stay this way forever. There was no guarantee he was headed toward safety; he debated asking the driver to turn back, but swallowed his nerves, refocusing on the windshield wipers, the driver's fragrant cinnamon-laced coffee, the lingering coconut cologne of a previous rider.

They drove for an hour down the interstate. The downpour slowed the traffic to a crawl. Between Saint Pluvia and New Harbor's vineyard coast, a sea of cars winked with thousands of off-rhythm hazard lights. Their flickering, bioluminescent.

He remembered a drunken stunt during a weekend in New Harbor: a joyride on a borrowed day cruiser. There had been posts on social media regarding jellyfish swarming a mile off the bay. Chanda had convinced her pet frat boy to steal his sleeping father's boat keys.

It was a radiantly humid July night, the moon a sliver and stars hidden behind clouds. The mayflies, the caddisflies, the damselflies, the dragonflies, the stoneflies, the lanternflies, all skidded the water's surface. Unseen katydids and crickets screamed with their wings.

Chanda stood beside her college fling, arm over his shoulder as he improvised at the wheel. Though Simón was happy for them, he wished he had someone to love. No matter: Chanda's relationship would be short-lived, partially due to the fallout from their excursion.

Five minutes out on the bay, the boat slowed.

"Holy fucking shit," Chanda whispered.

Below the cool obsidian shallows, the jelly bloom shimmered, hundreds of invertebrates blooming outward like supernovae. They floated under the boat and surrounded them with a slow-pulsing shine. Pink and blue as far as any of them could see. *The world can be so beautiful,* Simón remembered thinking then, *no matter how ruined I feel.*

Now, in the cab, the rainfall silenced almost everything. The traffic inched forward toward an accident on the shoulder.

The deer was whole and unbloodied. The driver that had killed it heaved the corpse further out from the road with his bare hands. Simón stared into those death-darkened eyes as the cab passed the wreckage. The traffic dispersed and the swarm of cars scattered.

He ruminated on the deer that had barreled through Roberta's show. The roadkill was too large to be the fawn, too small to be the mother. He ruminated on its broken body. The image haunted him like a looped track, the animal's departed soul joining billions of others killed by cars, ospreys tangled in strings, pigeons striking glass, then pavement. *It means nothing other than what it is,* he thought, attempting to nudge himself back down to earth.

The cab exited the highway and passed over hills, through golden leaf-lined streets, and out into torched vineyards — an attempt at beetle management, he supposed. A few blocks from the shore, the rain finally slowed to a drizzle.

Ma's house stood over a little hill high enough to see a small stretch of the bay, out past the manmade dunes and the brilliant crepe myrtles. This place was never Simón's home, a place Ma bought after he'd graduated and moved to Saint Pluvia, the next city over.

The cab idled by the curb as he sank his finger into the buzzer. A curtain pulled back from the bay window, and the door flung open.

"Simón!"

"Hey, Ma."

She eyed his suitcase. "You're soaked, get in here before you catch something."

"Actually…" He turned, pointing to the cab. "Could you, uh—"

She pursed her lips, annoyed. "Let me grab my purse."

Since he'd last visited a few months back, she'd repainted the walls in pastel shades more suited to egg decoration than interior design. Her sectional was plush white leather layered with swaths of fluffy sheepskin. It all appeared expensive: the glittering crystal knobs, the chrome-legged tables, the perfectly slick and level composite flooring.

In the kitchen, Ma dug into the depths of the pantry and the stainless-steel fridge, lining the silver-veined marble countertops with snacks.

"You could have called," she said.

"I lost my phone."

"When?"

"I don't know, maybe like a week ago?"

"And you haven't replaced it?"

"I lost my wallet, too."

"That explains the insane cab bill," she said.

Silence filled the room as Simón tore into a crinkly

pouch of animal crackers drenched in pink and white frosting. "Aren't you gonna ask if I got robbed?" he asked, nonpareils scattering everywhere.

"I figured you would've led with it. Don't chew with your mouth open. It makes you look like—" She cut herself off. Not Abi — he'd had impeccable table manners; she meant someone else she'd pushed away, maybe Simón's dad or her sister. No way to know without asking, and he'd already caused enough trouble for one day.

He swallowed dryly. She handed him a carton of orange juice, which he poured directly down his throat. His appetite was voracious, the strongest it'd been in ages.

"Whatever happened to cups?"

"You handed me the whole thing!" He laughed, clearing his throat.

She smiled in spite of herself. "So, the suitcase. Is this a seaside vacation or what?"

"Maybe a little more than that."

She pursed her lips. "No. Three nights max. That's it. My boyfriend is coming up this weekend."

"Your what?"

"I thought I told you about him. The guy from the app?"

"Ma, I got evicted."

"You're a grown man, Simón. You can't just run home every time you have a problem."

"When have I ever—"

"I'm just saying, that's not what I'm here for."

"Then what *are* you here for?" he asked.

She turned and gestured to the pristine, pale pink palace. "I'm here to live by the beach!" She pushed a container of pasta salad toward him. "And to feed you."

The mixed messaging made his head spin.

Something about the autumnal rains always made him miss his mother's cooking. No matter how broken their dynamic, the dinner table had served as a safe zone. Or, at least, a likely site for repair.

The pasta salad had flavorful cherry tomatoes Ma had grown herself. "Those are the only ones I managed to grow before the infestation," she said, wistful. "It was a mercy killing. Damn pink-spotted-beetles almost took my whole garden!"

She set a Tupperware of lemon chicken piccata before him, then returned to the fridge to see what else needed disposal.

"How about the asparagus bisque I had for lunch? With croutons?" He nodded, mid-chew. "It's been horrible out. I was thinking of making banana bread. You'll eat that, won't you?" He nodded again. "Good. You need to eat more, Simón. You're too skinny. I've been worried sick. I called and called, even before you lost your phone," she said.

The same old script. He braced himself for what would come next.

"You ignore your own mother, Simón," she said again. "Don't I deserve to know what's going on with you? Don't you ever miss me?"

"Of course I do," he surrendered. "Of course."

The dam between them weakened, then burst. Tears dampened her cheeks, pooling in the deepening lines. When had she gotten so old? When had he? He hugged her, rested his chin on the delicate yarn of her shoulder. Breathing in her reassuring floral perfume, Simón couldn't help but feel he'd betrayed himself.

That night, after Ma went to bed, Simón dug out a warm outfit from his disorganized suitcase before flicking off the guest room's overhead light and slipping down the creaky staircase and out the back door. The frigid night air heightened his senses. He hiked gingerly down the steep hill, toward the water.

Black waves rushed and shattered in the distance, indistinguishable from the velvet sky. The neighboring homes, primarily summer rentals, were dark and still. The road was devoid of parked cars. A squeal came from a whale-shaped weathervane, twisting atop a decrepit Victorian.

He thought he might walk along the coast, but as he approached and the crashing waves grew louder, the cruel wind stung his exposed flesh. His overgrown hair whipped his chapped face. His eyes watered and his nose leaked. *Fuck this*, he decided. Back up the hill he went.

Out of breath, he trudged up the stairs to find the guest room light on. His mother was surrounded by piles of his clothing.

"What the fuck is this?" she demanded, shaking an

orange bottle of Xanax.

"Why are you going through my shit?" He marched over to take it from her, but she yanked away.

"Who's Katrina Walsh? Let me guess, some stressed-out college student who pawned off her meds. You couldn't even bother to repackage it."

"What do you want me to say?"

"I don't know! Tell me your imaginary girlfriend accidentally left her meds in the bag before you borrowed it. Tell me my son isn't a junkie!" Her face contorted with outrage.

He groaned and slumped, face down, onto the pillowy white duvet. "You're totally overreacting," he hollered, voice muffled.

"Don't give me that teenage bullshit."

"It's not like I take 'em every day. It's just in case."

"Then get your own prescription!"

"You know I'm unemployed," he whined.

She shook her head. "Why does everyone think I'm an idiot?" More a statement than a question.

"Not an idiot," he mumbled. And then, even quieter, "Just nosey."

"Excuse me?"

Simón was silent.

"You better watch your tone. I have a right to know who you are, and what you're doing. The nerve to call me nosey — you're the one who showed up at my door unannounced, crying for help. I don't know why you hate me so much. All

I've ever done is try to help."

He shut his eyelids and let the pain return — the hurt was familiar, old, maybe even inherited. He spoke slowly and decidedly.

"You took a job at Innovore after I was fired. You took it to prove I was a failure. You pretended it meant nothing. You pushed me away. You... you—" he sputtered, unable to find the next words. His heart trilled like a snare drum. He ducked his head back into the pillow to calm himself, to hide the welling tears. The freshly washed pillowcase smelled of almond and vanilla.

"I quit, Simón." Her voice lowered, calm. "I work for their competitor now, Mint Aqua. I had that job for a month and couldn't stand all the lingo, ABC-bullshit. And I'm sorry you got your feelings hurt. But you wouldn't talk to me about any of it. And now..." She raised the prescription bottle in her hand, "you're still running away from your problems. For what?"

He didn't know how to reply. He rose to his feet, snatched the bottle from her hand, and rushed out the room to chuck it into the bathroom trash bin. "It's gone, okay? Happy?"

She stared, arms crossed, waiting for him to calm down.

"Why didn't you tell me you quit?" he demanded.

"Simón, I reached out dozens of times, but you wouldn't answer. You always complained about me ignoring your boundaries, so I tried to give you the space you wanted. Maybe if you'd answered the damn phone, you'd know I took that job because I missed you. I wanted to know what you went through. I wanted to understand you." She stepped closer to stroke his hair.

He nodded, quietly analyzing her defense strategy. It was almost impressive, the way she'd twisted her hurtful behaviors into unappreciated gifts. At his core, he knew the truth: she'd joined Innovore for the same reason she'd moved a short drive from his new city, the same reason she'd joined the swim team, the same reason she'd driven Dad away when he was just a toddler.

Despite everything, he needed her. The only option was reconciliation. He ceded.

"I'm sorry, Ma." And that was all it took. They hugged, and Simón went to bed.

He lay sleepless, annoyed that the Xanax had been wasted. While visiting the bathroom during the night, he checked the bin, and it was no longer there. Ma had likely moved it, buried it under other garbage elsewhere, never to be found again.

Morning came with more rain. After a multi-course breakfast, Simón and Ma visited a nearby phone store to purchase a replacement. When they returned home, Ma forced him to sit down at the kitchen table and complete the application for a new ID. She scoured the garage for a while, then handed him a turquoise Velcro wallet made for children with magnolia flowers printed on both sides. "It's all I could find. And here. Don't ask questions." She presented him with $200 cash and a check for enough to save him from immediate eviction.

"What's this, Ma?"

"Que hinchapelotas," she muttered with an almost imperceptible smile. "I said no questions. Pay your rent!"

Slowly, Simón slid the check and cash into the nylon wallet. It felt like lead in his pocket. From the living room, he could hear Ma slide open the curtains.

Ma had never given him so much money, not even for college. He'd screwed up, lost his job, burned through his savings. He was grateful for this bailout, truly, but ashamed. At the same time, he felt secure knowing that Ma was doing well for herself. She'd climbed the rungs to the middle class, to this bayside house, far from the life they'd lived before.

In the living room, Mary J. Blige played on the speaker system.

Simón hung his head and sighed. Couldn't she have helped him out when he needed it before? Why start now?

The next day, an unseasonable warmth spread underneath the dull vastness, replacing days of rain.

Simón woke up thinking about the shoreline and immediately reached for his sweatshirt. Ma was still asleep when he closed the front door behind him.

His eyes skirted across the lurching, littered tides, the cawing gulls above. Down by the water, countless, pink-spotted beetles rambled over the shore. He felt ready for the great reminder he was alive. Ready for a reunion with the shards of lost eons, for an answer to the mystery he'd unknowingly followed all his life. Ready to learn to use the key. Ready to resurface, stronger and wiser, purged of the burdens of work and home. The birdsong, and the tenuous promise of companionship and care, were all that remained. All he had was the past to remember and the future to fear. He wanted more. He wanted everything. It wouldn't come, he knew, but readiness was what mattered.

Starlings and beetles chased the ebbing tide. The gray immensity above, threads unwoven in the sky. He stripped off his socks and shoes, wading up to his calves into the frigid wash.

Drifting with the current, a mile-wide fishing net roped together hundreds of derelict soda cans, cigarette butts, food wrappers, and a trapped graveyard of jellyfish and pink-spotted beetles. It slipped into the distance, vanished into the mists.

Saltwater, cool on his face.

A forgotten conversation surfaced from the recesses of his adolescence — something shouted and whispered at once, overheard during one of his parents' final fights before the split.

How dare you use my father's films against me?

Abi never gave much detail about the films, beyond his pride in them. All Simón knew was that Ma and Cecilia had starred in some of them and held completely different relationships to the events. Cecilia was as proud as her father; Ma, secretive and pained. Simón had never mentioned the films to her at the risk of igniting her wrath.

Back at the house, he repacked his things and thanked his mother for all she'd given him: the food, the phone, the cash. But there was one more thing he needed.

Chrysalis

n the backseat of the cab, Simón clutched the bag full of Abi's films as coastal farmland turned to suburb.

At first, Ma had protested. "I don't recognize myself in those films, Simón." She paused, gathering strength. "When I was little, those movies took your Abi, my Pa, away from me. I don't think you're ready."

"I'm thirty, Ma. I should see them." He'd looked her in the eye. "Shouldn't I?"

And that was that. They rested, heavy in their tote bag, waiting to be witnessed.

The cab swelled with song, staccato violin climbing and gathering. Vivaldi's *Four Seasons*, now on "Autumn." The rosary strung from the rearview swayed with the dip and rise of the highway through ash-white birches. Simón felt the pale memory of wooden beads tangled through his fingers as Abi held him and prayed.

He examined the phone Ma bought; plastic film still plastered over the screen. It felt undeserved, like indispensable poison. In his jacket pocket, he found the crumpled paper with phone numbers listed in Roberta's messy scrawl. He'd had more friends once. Over a hundred contacts in his lost phone, though none of them felt necessary to replace. He took in the stripped-down social network — three numbers, excluding Ma's. What a small, strange web it was. And how bizarre that Roberta, a stranger just a couple weeks ago, was at the center. Some strands of the web were particularly fragile. He wasn't sure Chanda would even take his calls after he'd left things.

He considered messaging Chanda an apology for acting like a selfish asshole, but that meant confronting the truth: in his quest for meaning, he'd abandoned those who actually cared. He could just keep it casual, just ask to hang out, but it felt too soon. *Forget it.*

Roberta would be at work, he assumed, and he was hesitant to contact her after everything she'd said about traversing other worlds. The surreality of the conversation had made him uncomfortable.

Only Nausi remained. Simón couldn't imagine what they'd be doing at noon on Saturday. Probably not working, assuming they were a nine-to-fiver.

Hey, what are you up to? This is Simón, by the way. From the concert.

"Stupid," he mumbled to himself. He deleted the draft, stared out the window at the pine trees flitting past. He remembered what Nausi had said about their name. He searched for a digital image of the classic anime film and settled on Princess Nausicaä on her glider soaring above a post-apocalyptic wilderness.

Two minutes later, the message was marked as read. Five minutes later, Nausi still hadn't responded. Embarrassed, he added, *Sorry if that was awkward. I'm heading back to town from a trip. You free?*

He shut his eyes and leaned back, defeated, into the headrest.

Almost immediately, the phone buzzed.

I'm at home working, Nausi replied, then sent over an address. *Come by if you want.*

It didn't sound enthusiastic, but he couldn't handle returning to his doomed apartment.

"Excuse me?" Simón yelled over the music. "Any chance I can change the destination?"

Unseasonable warmth blanketed Simón as he exited the cab in front of Nausi's house. Innovore's glistening peak jutted above the treetops of this forested residential pocket of the Upper East Side.

He sunk his finger into the doorbell and waited. After a few long minutes, he texted, but his message couldn't be delivered. Abandoning his luggage on the stoop, he circled the home, peering into windows for signs of life. A plate with a half-eaten sandwich rested on the wooden kitchen table, waiting to be finished. On the opposite side of the house, a trail of debris led from the driveway dumpster to an open cellar door. Inside, a long ramp vanished into foreboding darkness.

"Hello?" he called, voice echoing.

He worried someone would think he was breaking in, but even the nearest neighbors were wholly obscured by dense foliage. A spark flashed from inside the basement, growing brighter by the moment, accompanied by an ethereal tune from the belly of the earth. He called out once more.

"Simón?" a voice called back.

"Is that you, Nausi?"

"Yeah, hang on a sec."

Preceded by the rattle of an overloaded wheelbarrow, Nausi emerged in a mud-splotched, pink, floral jumpsuit and black knee-high rubber boots, long dark hair gathered in a matching bandana, á la Rosie the Riveter.

"Whew," they exclaimed, "it's hot as hell up here."

"Want some help?" Simón offered.

"I'm fine!" They huffed and puffed, heaving the wheelbarrow up the ramp and into the daylight. Sunlight illuminated the contents of the cart: jagged wedges of brown stone surrounded by pebbles and soil.

"So, how's it going?" It felt like an absurd question to ask someone smeared with sweat and dirt, but he wasn't sure how else to break the ice.

"Not bad, just working on some stuff."

"Digging a basement pool?" he joked.

Nausi smiled but didn't laugh. "Something like that." They glanced at the dumpster with dread. "Maybe I could use a hand after all."

Simón followed them over to the driveway.

"I used to be able to just open these doors and tilt the barrow in, but it's too full for that now. Had to go bucket mode."

They handed him a crusty red bucket and instructed him to start scooping. The dumpster's contents mostly matched that of the wheelbarrow, but with more variation in dirt colors, as though Nausi had sampled several tiers of the earth's crust.

Together, they made quick work of the load. Nausi wiped their hands on the jumpsuit, satisfied.

"I suppose I should invite you in now," they said, almost a question.

"That'd be nice," Simón said, laughing. He remembered that this was his first fully sober experience of their hospitality and found their inelegance more endearing than off-putting.

"Right, yes." They unlocked the front door and gestured for him to enter. "I'll come in from the basement. Gotta keep the mud out."

He paced around the living room before a door in the kitchen swung open. Nausi emerged in a clean t-shirt and leggings. He smiled politely, then hesitated, unsure of what exactly to ask for, or how. He reverted to flattery. "I had a lot of fun with you the other night," he said.

"Good." And then, as if realizing they were supposed to say more, "I also had fun."

"Good. Good." He stared down at his feet, summoning courage. "I just came from my mom's house."

"Oh yeah?"

"Yeah. She's over on the coast. I don't like visiting, but I, uh, I didn't know where else to go. I'm having some problems. At my apartment."

Nausi opened the fridge to retrieve a pizza box, then gnawed on a stiff triangular slice. "What kind of problems?"

"Financial, mostly."

"Mostly?"

"And personal, I guess. I'm not sure I should be alone there anymore."

"Maybe you could get a roommate," they suggested.

"It's a one bedroom." He sighed. "Also, I don't know that I can trust a stranger right now."

"I'm a stranger."

"Not exactly," he said, looking around at the nostalgic decor. An oversized bottle stuffed with carefully arranged peppers and garlic cloves sat on the counter, raffia knotted around its neck. A dusty tin rooster perched proudly on the cabinets above. "I don't know why, but I feel like I can trust you."

"Thanks." Nausi's face softened. "I'd like to trust you too."

"I think you can."

"One way to find out."

Simón followed Nausi into the basement down a wooden staircase. Beside the washer and dryer, a wheelbarrow, a few stacked bags of concrete, and a sole table, surface littered with tools and papers.

An arch in the back wall framed a passageway with yet another set of steps. They descended in total silence, the damp coolness inviting them further and further in. He didn't dare make a sound. The cinder block walls were stained with trailing fingerprints. Simón dragged his hands along them as if deciphering hieroglyphics, trying to understand. A long wire trailed along the curve where the wall met the ceiling.

Earth weighed heavily overhead, and the entryway dimmed behind them with every step. Nausi's lantern ignited with a click, pushing away the darkness. Its glow refracted off pearlescent stone and reddish belts of subterranean teeth, jagged organs protruding from above. The passage widened, opening to a high-ceilinged atrium with branching channels. Nausi took out their lighter and held it to the wicked oil lamps mounted to the chamber's walls. Simón whistled with awe.

"What in the—"

The orange flickered off ancient planetary tissue, striated with age. Each fracture in the stone, a story, a dream chiseled out from the planet. The passage, unsanctioned by governing bodies, the product of madness or will. Someone — Nausi perhaps — had made this, had dreamed of carving out a burrow beneath Saint Pluvia and done it. Simón delicately touched the wall nearest him, as if pushing any harder would send him tumbling through the burgundy stone into a sea of magma moating the world's heart, dissolving him into toxic gas. The wall drummed, vivacious, up his forearm and into his shoulder and chest, matching his own heartbeat. He breathed in the sweet, almondine fragrance of the surrounding stone.

Before them, the atrium forked into three dark tunnels, each marked with a colorful swatch above their entrances: green, blue, yellow. A patch of ground beside the yellow tunnel sunk into a ghostly pool: a sump basin. Revving in its pale depths, a hosed pump respirated unholy water into ducts, which flowed into a system of tubes that passed through a gash in the ceiling.

Before he could ask about the oil lamps, Nausi explained that the wire he'd seen on the way in only provided enough electricity to power the energy-efficient pumps. He remembered earlier, the way Nausi had welcomed him from the basement, their lantern a slow roving beacon. He remembered the Butterfly Street sinkhole, how during his bender he'd seen a flashing light moments before losing his phone.

"Home sweet home," Nausi said. Their delivery was so flat that Simón couldn't tell if they were joking.

"You built this?" He spun in a circle, marveling at the subterrestrial miracle.

They had to be at least a few stories below ground. The initial passage from the windowless basement had been at least a hundred steps downward into the nave.

"Someone did, decades ago. Rum runners, probably. My parents just tapped into the network."

"Your parents?"

"Yeah, they were hobby tunnelers. They were just trying to build out a root cellar. But once they got going, it just became a fixation. I hated them for it, but now... I dunno. It's become my project too."

"Are you down here a lot?"

"Almost every day," Nausi said.

"What about work?"

"Well, after they died, there was a pretty big settlement. I get by just fine on that plus the occasional graphic design gig. Gives me plenty of time to work on this."

"Digging?"

"And reinforcing the structure, managing water, keeping the electrical running and air circulating, that kind of thing. I've had to teach myself plumbing, electrical, and most recently, HVAC." They motioned to ductwork combing the wall.

"It's unbelievable," Simón admitted. "But..."

"But?"

"But why? I mean I know why your parents got into it, but why keep it going? What's it all for? This must've been years and years of work."

Nausi shrugged. "There's probably some psychological reason," they said, "but, mostly, it's because I forget about everything else when I'm here. I'm alone. Sometimes, I can hear the world digesting. It's like I'm in the gears of a machine."

Nausi walked from lamp to lamp, extinguishing flames.

They kept speaking as though nothing had changed.

Simón startled as Nausi's warm hand groped for his elbow.

"Are you afraid of the dark?" they asked, pulling him closer. The shape of their voice was round and reassuring.

Drops of water plinked in the untraceable distance.

He recalled the glowing plastic nightlight Ma plugged into the outlet across from his racecar bed. "I was," he said.

It was night by the time they resurfaced, flushed and giddy. The shared orgasm had diffused the layer of tension that had clung to him since discovering the eviction notice. Nausi had invited him to stay the night, and they'd eaten the remaining slices of stale pizza before piling into the twin bed upstairs.

"Tomorrow, I'll go to the bank and cash the check," he announced dispassionately, chin resting atop Nausi's head.

"What check?"

He exhaled, then against all impulses, unloaded on Nausi: the end of his contract, the depleted checking account, the months of unpaid rent, the foreboding letter taped to his door, and the fat check decorated with his mother's looping signature. "The crazy part is I don't even want to go back," he said, at last. "It doesn't feel like home anymore."

Nausi had propped themself up on their elbows for the

duration of Simón's saga. "Then don't," they said, as though it were the simplest fact imaginable.

"Don't?"

"Don't go back. Don't pay the back rent."

Visions of the aftermath danced across his vision: the court appearance, the clumsy public defender, his possessions piled on the sidewalk for anyone to claim or destroy, his mother's unfettered fury about the avoidability of it all. But when he pulled back from the fear, when he imagined the liberation the purge would inspire, all was awash with relief. It was like passing beneath a mister at a theme park in the roasting heat of summer — the crisp moment when a hot breeze meets dewy flesh.

"But where would I go? My mom said—"

"Here." Nausi snuggled in closer, their voice almost a whisper. "Here."

In the Labyrinth

Simón began to dream in crisp, unprecedented detail. In one, Roberta chases him into the tunnels without a lantern until a wet, muddy mouth swallows them whole. In another, he is Chanda's mangled pigeon, splayed out on the table as she slowly stitches him, weeping into the raw wound. In another, a young Abi chases Ma and Tía Cecilia through a field of flowers with an 8mm camera, a field that ends in a steep cliff. Abi films their doomed descent, then turns to Simón, closer and closer until the lens presses, cold, against his eye.

The dreams spilled out, coated the waking world with a hypnagogic sheen. Something had invited surreal visions — the sudden sobriety, or his daily descent underground. Upon waking, he'd walk past Ma's uncashed check, out to the hall bathroom to try washing off the disorientation. Then, to the kitchen to cook. With only a little cash to contribute to Nausi's pizza fund, meal prep felt like the best way to thank his host, who lacked any semblance of culinary inspiration. Channeling Ma, Simón concocted amateur but hearty meals, warming their bellies, and providing the strength they needed to tunnel.

When he wasn't cooking, he was in the basement with Nausi, shoveling and picking at the hard, dense earth, transporting shatters and stone clods with the wheelbarrow. It was impossible to know the scope and scale of the operation below the home.

After one particularly long day in the reception-less underground, Simón emerged to a voicemail from Ma, demanding to know why he hadn't cashed the check. He blamed his lack of identification, which would take at least another week to arrive at the old apartment. She insisted he contact his landlord to explain the delay and he promised he would, knowing fully well that he wouldn't.

Apart from Ma's intrusions, life with Nausi, strange as it was, had stabilized his routine in a way he'd once feared impossible.

The heatwave resuscitated summer from its sleep. Nausi's front lawn browned, every tree undressed, and the butterflies and bees surged around the dwindling flowers in the yard. Not a single cloud pocked the sky.

It'd been three, maybe four nights. He counted on his fingers. *Wait, it's been five.* He didn't want to leave but couldn't help keeping a guilty tally. He didn't want to jinx it by asking how long he could stay, assuming Nausi would mention it themself.

There was a peculiar stasis in the cool underground, one that made his days run together. Sometimes, his palms pushed against stone walls for reassurance. *Nothing here can hurt you.* Even with all his weight heaving against it, the earth held strong. No burgundy curtain. Just dirt, layers, and layers, and atop all that dirt, Saint Pluvia — his adopted home, his beautiful metropolis whose lungs dripped poison, whose vessels clogged with plaque, who's all-seeing-eye degraded its own children.

An unusual paradise, without question. Everything had a sweetness to it. The way Nausi wordlessly hauled stone from wall to wheelbarrow. Their tacit collaboration above ground and below, a shared understanding not to break each other's focus. These quiet hours allowed glances, smiles, sometimes a kiss; but, for the most part, there was work to be done.

From Nausi's bedroom, Simón had noticed mint leaves flourishing in the unkempt patch of garden beneath the window. Bouquets of rich green leaves bundled to thick stems, crowding out the drooping sunflowers, the fading echinacea. Now, in the kitchen, he strained his eyes against the overhead lights, pupils fussing like a camera lens after so many hours in the black of the tunnels.

The rusted kettle hissed in Simón's hands. Scalding water gurgled into a large orange thermos that might have belonged to Nausi's family's camping repertoire two decades ago. He gathered a handful of mint leaves, freshly washed, and dipped them into the thermos with a long spoon. He stirred a coin of honey into the steeping brew.

Who was this tea drinking, meal prepping, tunnel digging man who'd overtaken his body? This wasn't some earlier, abandoned version of himself. No, this was someone entirely unfamiliar. Whoever the man was, Simón respected him. Liked him, even.

He placed the thermos inside Nausi's old backpack alongside a bag of pretzel sticks.

Downstairs, Nausi waited by the tunnel's mouth, a headlamp strapped to their forehead. They dangled a second headlamp from their thin finger. Simón bowed his head to let Nausi crown him, the elastic band gripping his temples. Nausi stepped softly into the planet's exposed vein and Simón followed.

They left the tools on their hooks. No excavating this evening. It was time to explore. "To *witness*," Nausi said.

Soon they were swallowed by darkness, the beams of the headlamps like two bouncing moons. Their synchronized footsteps reverberated off the tunnel walls, blending with the lively drip and churn of unseen water. He felt sucked into a living system, more biology than geology.

Simón and Nausi traveled the sloping grade to the wide chamber where the paths diverged. They paused, bathed in the darkness. Every shallow breath, every scuff of stone resounded.

In the lamplight, Nausi reached into a pocket and unfolded a small, detailed map. Hand-drawn with the precision of a master cartographer, it seemed to be an underground blueprint of the city. The labyrinthine network held dozens of interconnected channels.

"Here," Simón said, poking a point on the map. "That's where my apartment is. And right there, that's the sinkhole.

At the end of the blue route?"

Nausi nodded, pressed their lips into a proud smile.

"And no one else knows about this," he said, a realization more than a question.

"I've never encountered another person, but someone had to know about it, at some point. I've found all kinds of trash from different eras — broken stoneware crocks, old Coke bottles, cigarette butts, a little drug paraphernalia. Seems like the city sealed off all the entrances sometime in the last fifty years. But someone's gotta remember. It's hard to seal off a rumor."

They pressed deeper into the tunnels than Simón had ever been. Nausi kept the map handy, and Simón glanced over occasionally, trying to grasp where they were. He wondered how long it would take to reach the end of each pathway. He wondered if the map was complete; how endless was this other world, this city beneath the city, and were there more worlds nestled within? Were there other universes waiting while he struggled in the bright, loud world above? *Is this what Roberta meant?* "So, I wanted to ask about something you said. Back at Roberta's show—"

"What?" Nausi had caught him off guard. He wondered if he'd been thinking out loud. "Sorry, go on."

"Okay," Nausi continued. "So, when we met, my friends and I asked you about your album. But you were pretty cagey about it. I guess I'm just wondering what the deal is. Is it a secret?"

"Not really." He was surprised by the sudden interest.

"You just never asked again."

"Was I supposed to?"

"I don't know. It's nothing. I don't think it's even art."

"Right, you said you were... exploring something."

"Yeah. After my job ended, I was alone for a long time. It was bad. Really bad. Chanda finally got me to go out on this bird watching excursion. I brought all my old audio stuff. I don't know why. Maybe it was a security blanket," he admitted. "Anyway, I found this isolated little clearing and there was a strange sound. Probably just a bird. But it *felt* like something more."

The resonance of his own voice, enclosed in the vacuum of the tunnel, made him self-conscious. Nausi listened intently, reassuringly. He continued.

"When I listened to the recording later, I heard my name, clear as day. But there was no one else around. It had to have been the bird. I know I sound crazy, but Roberta heard it in the track too. And now, I have these other recordings and — I swear on every bone in my body — there are more messages. Messages *designed* for me." The story sounded impossible, even to him. He braced himself for Nausi's rejection.

"Hold on," Nausi said. They stopped walking and turned their light on Simón's face. "So, Roberta heard a message."

"Right." Simón squinted against the white light.

"The same exact message that you heard."

"I guess so, yeah."

"Did she repeat it back to you?" Nausi folded their arms and waited for Simón's response.

Simón paced around Nausi, scratching the back of his neck. "I guess not. But Roberta said—"

"Roberta says a lot of things, Simón. I think you know that by now. The woman is a legend, but she's also, you know..."

"Yeah, I know."

"It doesn't mean it's not a worthwhile project. You should keep at it. Don't let all this cooking and tunneling distract you." They waited a moment and self-corrected. "It's not that I don't appreciate your help. It's been great, but I don't want you to feel obligated. I want you to settle in, make time for your own things."

He allowed their words to sink in before responding. "Thanks, Nausi. Yeah, maybe I will."

They advanced through the blue tunnel for what felt like hours until reaching another womb-like vault of diverging aisles. Channels only wide enough for one, and they'd have to proceed in succession with each other. The entrances loomed, unmarked. He looked back at Nausi.

"Go ahead," they said. "Choose a path."

Nausi followed him down the central branch, tracing the newfound route with a pencil. Snacking on pretzels, they continued for at least a mile. Then, out of nowhere, Nausi yelped and Simón's legs went cold. Shock seared through his body as Nausi's headlamp caught on the water's obsidian surface.

"It's freezing," he shouted.

Nausi shrieked again. They both waded, laughing, to the edge and clawed up the steep slope, looking back at the rippling water.

Twin beams of light bounced off the hidden lake. Everything outside the rays meshed into sameness.

"I don't know how we missed it." Nausi chuckled.

Later, they restored themselves with a home-cooked dinner of gazpacho and garlic bread. Nausi moved slowly while doing the dishes, happy but sapped of energy. Simón, on the other hand, was unusually alert. Nausi's insistence that he resumes his creative work had him thinking about the tunnel system's soundscape. And, in the background, the nagging question of what Roberta had actually heard in the birdsongs. He'd texted her about it as soon as he'd returned to the surface. No response yet. To alleviate his anxiety, he asked Nausi if, before going to bed, they would listen for messages in the original files.

"*You* could tell me if it's real," he said.

"I don't think I should," they said. "Those messages are for you. You don't need mine, or Roberta's, or anyone's confirmation to know what's true."

When Nausi went to bed, he adjourned to the wainscoted den. While retrieving his laptop, he spotted the tote bag of VHS tapes sitting untouched in the corner.

The tapes were old, and the films stored on them, even older. Abi had made the majority when he was around Simón's age, later converting to VHS to preserve his own legacy. If only Abi had known how short the shelf life of his chosen format was.

Simón knew Ma loathed the films, but it seemed she was in the minority. An archived Web 1.0 article said the works had sent shockwaves through the art world when screened. Galleries and museums had repeatedly reached out to Ma, the sole executor of Abi's estate, for permission to curate them, and she'd always declined, despite Cecilia's pleading. In Ma's iron grip, the films receded from the public realm entirely. Simón had no idea what to expect.

Beneath the television, the VCR's digital clock flashed. He selected the tape with the earliest marked date, labeled in Abi's sharp, miniscule handwriting. *Experimentos, 1962–1978.*

One end of a converter went into the VCR's port, and the other into his laptop, set delicately on the carpet. Simón crossed his fingers that the tape still worked, then guided it into the machine.

Whirs and clicks, lines of gray and white static vibrating across the screen. He tapped the spacebar to start the transfer. A poorly rendered blue graphic in a blocky font announced the first film's title:

The Whale's End (El Final de la Ballena)

Fade in. Seaweed crusted with sand.

Piano chords strike among softly buzzing fields of guitar feedback.

The camera rises to reveal a beach packed with sunbathers in high-waisted swimsuits. Scintillating red and black specks flash across the screen. The camera pans slowly, trailing over a pale, almost gray ocean licking silently at the sand. The camera rounds to Abi's right, then comes to rest on stripes of white, a cage of bone. Sea birds tear away at remaining fragments of cartilage.

Quieter and quieter, piano chords bury themselves in the amassing feedback.

The camera lingers uncomfortably, then begins a tedious zoom out. A whale's skeleton coming fully into view, and then, an expressionless woman mirroring the massive, curving spine, body twisted in tandem. Her face is familiar but she's too old to be Ma. She sprinkles herself with something from a little bag, mouthing unknowable words.

The gulls' heads spin toward her. Within seconds, they've collectively abandoned the carcass and engulfed her entirely, leaving nothing but a pair of kicking feet jutting out from the swarm. Fade to black.

His grandmother, one of the only topics more sensitive than Abi, had up until now only existed in still images: flirting with the man behind the camera, cradling Simón's mother and aunt as pudgy infants. The circumstances of her death were still unknown to him; Ma would burst into tears any time she tried to explain. All he knew was that Abi had been solely responsible for rearing his daughters from at least the time Ma and her sister were school-aged, and that Ma acted like Abi was to blame for it all: the loss of their mother and the trauma that followed.

He checked the laptop. No errors yet. He paused the tape, saved the file, then restarted the reel.

The Halo (El Nimbo)

Fade in. A long neighborhood road stretches out. Golden hour illuminates landscaped yards, flowerbeds of petunias and hydrangeas, sleek cars in driveways, perfectly parallel.

The camera drops on a pair of cockroaches on the sidewalk, forced into battle. A fire poker, gripped in a child's hand, thrusts at the warriors, urging them closer.

Layered, distorted laughter dissolves into gentle acoustic guitar, the same song Abi had played at one of Simón's birthday parties.

Cut to a pair of patent leather shoes grinding shriveled earthworm corpses into the cement.

The camera lifts to the child's face for the first time: Cecilia, barely kindergarten aged, grins, then turns away, skipping into the distance, arms swinging.

Her silhouette, cast across the pavement, the exact likeness of a bird in flight. Fade to black.

Simón sipped his tea. It was clear why the films were well-received at the time. The sound design was ahead of its time, and the editing was impressive. They were symbolic, but in a way that anyone could understand; their meanings mostly based on emotion. They were episodic, short and sweet yet rich with detail. He saved the file, then moved on to the next.

Swim Lessons (Lecciones de Natación)

Darkness and splashing. Fade in.

A small child — Ma, no doubt — attempts to swim in a bathtub. Her limbs flail, and she lifts her face to gasp for air. The water grows dark and murky. Her body drips with black grease. The oil splatters against the pink bathroom tile, stains her yellow swimsuit, climbs up her cheeks. She sits up, rests her palms against blackened eyes, and opens her mouth to scream. Slack-jawed with dark saliva stretched between her open lips, the girl emits an engine's cry, the churning grind of a car failing to start. Fade to black.

The guttural wail continues for five, ten, twenty seconds. Then, at last, silence.

Simón paused the tape, heart pounding in his chest. *Jesus fucking Christ.* In the gaps between his horror, his mind flooded with questions — how could Abi do this to his own daughter? And what was the point of putting a child through that kind of stunt? There was no denying that art was impactful; it rattled him to his core. But despite its obvious environmentalist message, the work ethics were questionable at best. It was a miracle Ma's eyesight wasn't permanently damaged. With his grandparents dead, Cecilia an inflexible defender of the arts, and Ma too wounded to discuss the matter, there was no way to gain any real clarity on the presence of consent. Then again, there was no way a child could consent to motor oil in her eyes and mouth.

He hovered over the save button. To transfer the film would be to preserve it in amber forever. It would safeguard Abi's legacy for later generations. But to conserve the work would also be a dismissal of his mother's pain, a hand extending relentlessly into the future. For all the times she'd outpaced him — at checkers, on the swim team, even at Innovore — some miserable part of himself wanted to punish her, wanted to play *Lecciones de Natación* on an eternal loop just to spite her.

"Cancel" wouldn't delete the original video, he reassured himself. It'd just negate the import. The film would live on a while longer on cassette, degrading year by year until the tape crumbled entirely, bodily, into dust.

The reek of motor oil lingered in his nostrils long after shutting his computer down. That would be it for the night.

His phone vibrated; finally, a response from Roberta.

heard my nam. u hear urs? quantum shit!

Simón raised an eyebrow. He'd forgotten what an awful texter she was. He responded:

You heard your name? What's "quantum shit?"

After a few minutes of typing and retyping, she responded: *diff worlds. diff dimensions. we each have one vision of truth! but all share something bigger. u cracked it wide open. keep going keep going keep going*

He considered this a moment before another text came in.

g2g i'm tripping tn at echo bend. security asshole will have two cuff me 2 keep me out. btw down two collab if u want. with album or w/e is next.

＊

He crawled into Nausi's small bed around one in the morning, wrapping his arms around them. They stirred, then scooted against the wall, batting him away.

"Too hot."

He rolled over, pressing his back to theirs, and tried to fall asleep. But his mind raced with fighting roaches and terrified children. "Nausi?"

"Mm."

"I watched Abi's films."

"Huh?"

"I watched the tapes my mom gave me."

"Okay."

The fridge hummed in the distance.

"I finally understand why my mom hates him. I don't think— I don't think I got the same version of him that she got. It's like, I got the cameraman, and she got the lens."

Nausi sighed and rolled back to face him, rubbing their bleary eyes. "What're you talking about?"

"My grandpa."

"Well, can you just call him because I'm trying to sleep right now."

"He's *dead*."

"Okay."

"It's actually a pretty sensitive topic for me," Simón said.

"I don't know what you want me to say. Old men do that, Simón. They die. And honestly, if you're looking for sympathy about dead family members, you're barking up the wrong tree." Nausi sat up suddenly and crawled over him.

"Where are you going?" he asked.

"Turning on the goddamn AC."

"Can't you just crack a window?"

"It's hot out there too."

"But it's expensive."

"It's my house," they said, and with that, marched off to adjust the thermostat.

ƺ

The next morning, Simón started editing tracks. He'd decided to take their advice, devoting the entire day to his own project while Nausi attended to the basement. At first, he'd protested "wasting" the air conditioning by enjoying it in their absence, but Nausi insisted.

"Stop worrying about me. Please."

Their tone, just short of aggravated, told Simón not to push it. And so, while Nausi ventured underground, he made himself comfortable at the kitchen table.

Simón transformed, modified, and organized strata of sound. Measure upon measure, he parsed samples from field recordings, various digital archives, his old capstone work, and Abi's films — exhuming notes from the squeal of car tires, or the weathering of his old apartment walls, or birdsong. The extracted notes were stretched, reversed, and filtered, their idiosyncrasies peeled apart, hidden, or exposed. He slipped steadily into oblivion, into the embrace of all-consuming focus. Taking influence from Blasphemous Simulation of Love, he added a bass drum and a ton of reverb. He dreamed of adding organic instrumentation for a more human touch, whenever he had access to a guitar again. With each new layer, Simón's hand-crafted world grew increasingly ornate. After several weightless hours, hunger finally obstructed his flow. He checked the time; it'd somehow gotten to almost four-o-clock. He untangled himself from the posture he'd pretzeled himself into and rose onto tingling feet.

A green aura filtered through the windows, casting a disquieting specter over the kitchen. Pollution, no doubt. Simón grabbed a box of rotini and a jar of marinara from the freshly stocked pantry and filled a pot with water. The clang of steel on stovetop and the clicking burner seemed louder than usual, and when Simón stepped back to watch the water boil, he stood in silence. It wasn't just the chartreuse haze that unsettled him, he realized. It was the near-total absence of sound. An autumn afternoon should be sprinkled with squirrel chatter and birdsong, incessant communication about the impending freeze, turf wars, looming predators. Simón heard nothing.

He opened a window to be sure. The silence was so loud it made his ears ring, and the heatwave's scorch had been replaced with acute cold. Simón peered up and down the side yard. Not a creature in sight.

He sent Chanda a simple text: *Is it green where you are, or am I seeing shit?*

He paced, waiting for the water to boil, then turned to the internet, searching phrases like "neighborhood squirrels gone" and "weird light." Just as he'd begun to give up on finding an answer, Chanda's name flashed across his vibrating phone.

A mix of excitement and anxiety roiled in his empty stomach. It had easily been two weeks since she'd begrudgingly dropped him off at South Millipede Plaza. It both felt like yesterday and like an entire lifetime.

"What the ever-loving fuck, Simón!"

Simón took a moment to absorb the blow. "Good to hear from you."

"Oh please. Don't act like I'm the one who fell off the side of the planet. You straight-up disappeared. Again. Where the fuck have you been?" She sighed heavily.

Simón pictured her rubbing her temples, a classic Chanda move.

"It's…" He paused, breathed into the phone. "It's kind of hard to explain." He expected Chanda to snap back at him again. Instead, her voice softened.

"Are you okay? I've been really worried."

"I'm pretty good, actually. Thanks. I've been hiding out from the heatwave on the upper east side of town."

"At some girl's house?"

"Not a girl. Just Nausi."

"Right," Chanda said. "Well, since you've got a phone again, maybe you could try to actually keep in touch?"

"I'll try. I could use an old friend these days. Everything feels extra weird lately. The heatwave, this weird light…"

"Yeah. It's making everyone look nauseous. Wanna see something else?"

Chanda's fingernails tapped against the screen and his phone buzzed against his ear, indicating the arrival of a new message. The photo, zoomed and cropped, was blurry and pixelated, but appeared to show a flock of backlit birds soaring over Echo Bend.

"It's a *really* unusual murmuration. Saw it while rescuing another busted up pigeon in the park."

"What's so weird about it?"

"It's not so crazy to have a mixed species flock, but I've never seen size variation like this. You've got your typical flocking birds, like starlings, and then you got some that don't play well with others. Like hawks, owls."

"Aren't owls nocturnal?"

"Told you it was weird."

"I wonder if there's any precedent for this. Maybe the other birders know."

"Maybe," Chanda said. "But I dropped out of the club

a few days after you came for dinner. Between everyone enabling the neighborhood menace"— he could almost hear her shaking her fist at Roberta through the phone — "and a general disinterest in my pigeon rehab or the window sticker campaign, I started getting bitter. They don't give a fuck about birds. They just wanna own binoculars. Perverts. I've got bigger fish to fry. I'm up to six pigeon patients now. I've been looking for a bigger space." She lowered her voice to a whisper. "Don't tell anyone, but I'm thinking about quitting my job and starting a nonprofit rescue. Terrance thinks I'm going insane." She let out an ornery, contagious cackle.

It felt good to laugh together. Perhaps she was still quietly resentful of how he'd treated her. But it seemed they'd reached enough of a truce to have a laugh, which meant everything.

"Crazy is as crazy does," he offered.

"You would know."

The pot on the stove began to boil over.

Another strange, silent hour passed as Simón ate and returned to his editing. His phone buzzed, displaying a severe weather warning, but nothing had changed outside. Finally, shortly after sunset, Nausi's cart squealed in the sunken distance, signaling their return. Once upstairs, they tore into the cold leftover pasta without a word, ravenous.

He showed Nausi the photo Chanda had sent. They just nodded, unmoved. At the close of his long-winded anecdotes about the green sky and the missing squirrels, they replied dryly.

"Wow, that's wild."

He got the sense that they just wanted to get back underground.

"This storm could undo a whole summer's worth of work," they complained.

It didn't seem an appropriate time to mention his music. "I could—"

"I'm all set," they said. "Promise. It's dangerous down there if you don't know what you're doing."

Simón looked out of the window, at Nausi, at the table. "I'm just trying to be helpful."

They let out a long sigh. "I mean, if you truly wanna come, I guess I can't stop you."

Nausi deposited their dish in the sink, then returned to the tunnels, leaving Simón alone.

Reluctant to go to bed, he stayed awake editing audio and drank nearly two whole bottles of Nausi's parents' vinegary old wine. The first bottle lifted the shroud of sadness. The second replaced it with an aimless frenzy that led him out the front door.

Cool wind rushed through his hair. The aura was gone, supplanted by the storm. Soggy maple leaves cushioned his lurching steps. He opened his mouth to taste the rain cold on his tongue. Above, night's clouds rouged, angry and alive, blood rushing to their faces. The flashing sky tore open; heaven's rivers gushed to earth. Simón surrendered himself to it entirely, grateful for a break from the searing heat.

Shadow cloaked a tall bare elm across the yard. Simón stumbled toward it, desperate to caress the trunk. *Nothing here can hurt you.* His hands slid down the mottled bark. He sat on the slick roots, against the elm's trunk, scanning the heaving horizon through leafless, rain-darkened branches. Thunder croaked a demonic decree. In the distance, the Innovore tower stood indifferent. Its glass scales wore emerald moonlight, deepened by the green of signal lights. Raindrops glazed Simón's cheeks, his lips. The wind whipped him into hypnosis. Again, the clouds gasped and cracked. An electric vein opened, firing a strike above the towers.

Innovore's spire winked green one final time. A power outage, perhaps. Then, bolts struck the tower again and again. A great rumbling vibrated the ground.

Maybe it was the wine, but Simón believed every last window shattered in the bridge-linked towers. Down the crepuscular glass showered, like snow to dead earth. The wind blew harder, freeing the droplets that clung to branches above him, soaking him.

He thought of Nausi, toiling away beneath him. They'd said they didn't want help and he was inclined to respect that. But they'd also invited him to capture some subterranean recordings.

It was as good an excuse as any.

Murmuration

ain drummed against the windows of Nausi's bedroom. Blurred figures stared down from the posters plastering the walls. Simón sloppily transferred the contents of his gear bag into Nausi's old backpack, stripping down his setup to the bare essentials: the recorder, a couple mics, a collapsible tripod, and a pair of headphones. Digging into the depths of the gear bag, his hand brushed over a smooth lump at the bottom: his old leather wallet.

Thunder crashed in the distance. Simón laughed in disbelief. This whole time. It had been there the whole time. He stopped laughing when he recalled the old homeless woman he'd suspected of robbing him. It'd been pure paranoia; if he'd really thought about it, he'd have realized how ridiculous the theory was. How could a sickly old woman pickpocket him from three feet away? All she'd wanted was a taste of his relief. Where was she now? Did she have shelter from the harsh wind? Her words rang in his ears: *You're a selfish young man!*

He slung the backpack over his shoulders and turned off the bedroom light. In the basement, he slipped into a spare pair of Nausi's rainboots, and with a deep breath, descended into the basement. He grabbed a rechargeable lantern off the work bench, glancing blearily at the schematic beside it. The blue channel was somewhere in the right fork after the tunnel's entrance; right, then right, then right again. *Shouldn't be too difficult.* He traced muddy footprints to the archway carved into the basement's cinder block wall, then down the stone staircase into the atrium. Yellow flames danced atop the oil lamps, sending traces of soft light down each of the four main arteries: red, yellow, blue, green. He whistled as he entered the blue tunnel — a signal they'd agreed on after one too many startling incidents — Nausi didn't respond.

Still too far away. He'd try again in a couple hundred yards.

Most of the tunnel was narrow, just wide enough to accommodate a minecart and tall enough to walk without smacking one's head on the cast concrete ceiling. Water rushed in the distance. Around a corner was a generous cut-out in the wall — space enough should one need a break from excavation — and a sewer cover on the floor. A PVC pipe extended from a hole in the cover and vanished into the wall above it.

The sump pit, he realized, recalling one of Nausi's lectures about underground water management. This was one of five total sump pumps, one per channel and another near the entry point. *Not enough to keep everything dry, but better than nothing,* they'd said. The main barrier was electricity, followed by maintenance. The more sump pumps, the more likely that one would be broken at any given time. And extending electricity into the full depths of each tunnel would be a massive undertaking, one that would undoubtedly derail Nausi's expansion project. Simón had to give it to them: they were wholly devoted to the vision, whatever that vision was.

He set up his tripod and attached the shotgun mic, pointing the barrel at the pit to capture the aquatic gush and burble. He lowered himself onto a rusty folding chair, as still as possible to preserve the sound's purity. Simón fought the urge to yawn or shift to a more comfortable position. An untold number of minutes passed as he sank into his own drunken psyche.

Amid flashing images of everyone he'd encountered leading up to this folding chair was his grandmother, posed beside the whale carcass for Abi's steady camera. Abi, a man who knew exactly what he wanted and how to get it, a man whose ability to express himself in art outpaced his ability to protect his wife from death, his daughter's eyes from motor oil, or his grandson's smallness from gravity. Selective wisdom had cursed them both. He thought of Chanda, wished he had enough reception to call her again, to apologize properly for the imbalance of care, to donate his mother's check to her nascent bird rescue. It killed him that she'd responded after all his neglect. She was too forgiving of him, he realized with discomforting certainty.

The worst thing is, I don't deserve it.

He licked his lips. Saline. He'd been crying. He opened his eyes and found the world unchanged. He stopped the recording; twenty minutes had eclipsed without warning. Time worked differently down here. He shook himself loose from the strangeness, loaded his equipment back into the backpack, then set off back down the main tunnel, inching closer and closer to Nausi.

He walked for a long time, the route growing wetter and muddier with every step. Runoff sloshed over the toes of his borrowed rain boots. He paused to whistle, then held still, waiting for a response. Nothing but the flush of water. *Can the tunnels even handle flooding like this?* he wondered, whistling again. Then, somewhere ahead, a high-pitched tone. Their response filled him with relief. There had been an unpleasant moment — a fleeting millisecond of dread — where he'd imagined them crushed by falling rock.

Their signal reassured him, not just that they were unharmed, but that they wanted to be found.

Rainwater dripped onto itself, tinkling chimes. The pooling rose higher. Larger chunks snapped off the ceiling and plopped nearby, spraying him. The tunnel walls were slick, fracturing. Streams breached, joining the deluge. All he could do was splash forward.

The lantern flickered, then strengthened. Cold flood water filled his boots and a white wisp of light shone ahead. The path tilted uphill toward a drier patch, where Nausi stood on a stepladder surrounded by rubble and splintered debris, a blue bandana over their mouth and nose.

"Hey!" Simón yelled. "What the hell is happening?" Rushing water and the racket of construction continued. He was jogging now, or as near to jogging as the flooding allowed.

The tunnel was alive with sound, even without the pounding. Nausi pulled down the bandana and rested their sledgehammer against their shoulder.

"It's not safe down here," they shouted.

The wooden support beams upholding the ceiling had rotted and collapsed. Nausi had pulled much of it aside and was hammering long pieces of rebar into pre-drilled holes in the rocky walls and ceiling.

A clump of rock the size of a toaster oven tumbled from the ceiling, pebbles raining down in its wake. Simón shielded his head with his hands, and Nausi sped into action, pounding another piece of rebar into the wet stone.

Simón spun his lantern around. Behind him, the water he'd just passed through was rising fast. Straight ahead, an abrupt end to this branch of tunnel. Nausi had been extending it, but at this distance from the house, excavation was excruciating work. To Simón's right, another wing stretched into complete darkness.

"Let me help you," Simón yelled. The maelstrom of water had swelled to an unceasing roar. "Please, just tell me what to do."

"I don't need your help." Nausi's gaze was nailed to

their work — the rows of two-inch holes, the wheelbarrow piled with rebar. "There's no time to teach you."

"I'll figure it out, just let me try," Simón pleaded.

"This is extremely delicate work. If I don't reinforce this wall correctly, I'll lose months of progress. Now please, let me finish." Simón didn't move. Clearly agitated, Nausi continued. "I care about you, Simón. I do. But this?" They waved around their sledgehammer, gesturing to the entirety of their subterranean universe. "This is what I need to take care of. Right now, you need to take care of yourself. I can't do that for you now."

The fissure, the new distance between them, suddenly came into focus. The way they'd come to rely on each other for food and shelter, the way he'd taken their work on instead of pursuing his own. The way Nausi had been happily doing it all without him for years.

"What's that way?" He pointed down the dark branch to the right.

"I've been down there once. Super tight passage. But it leads to the surface."

Simón stared into its depths. There was no guarantee it would be safe, but the possibility tempted him. It wasn't totally submerged, at least.

"Come with me," he yelled. His voice cracked.

Turning away from Simón, Nausi pounded another rod into the wall. A long splinter sheared up from the hole, freeing a fist sized chunk of rock that crashed into the ground and rolled back toward the rising water. Nausi climbed down to retrieve another steel bar.

"Nausi!" Simón approached the stepladder and forced himself in front of them. "It's not working. The stone is too brittle. You're gonna get hurt, or worse."

"I don't care," they shouted. They tossed aside the sledgehammer with a clatter, glaring at him. "I know what I'm doing. Just worry about yourself. I'll meet you in a bit."

Simón clenched his fists. Righteous electricity surged through him. He wanted to force them, to grab them by the arm and sprint together toward the exit. Nausi's convictions were relentless, despite trembling eyes that betrayed a paralyzing panic. He reached out to touch them, to ground them, to capture their trust with his care. But they dodged his swipe and went to retrieve their mallet.

He watched them a moment longer: the acute focus on their face, the wild detachment in their eyes, the crazed flutter of futile tools. And then, in surrender, he turned toward the other channel, into the shadows.

Nausi understood. He corrected himself: *Nausi understands.* He told himself they were only a short while behind him. But how could they not leave with him? How could they care so little about their own wellbeing? Why wouldn't they listen when he begged to help?

As the earth steepened, Nausi's pounding grew muffled. Water seeped in all around him, pouring downslope. Ahead, iridescent stone sparkled in time with his flickering lantern's swing. Beyond that, dense shadow.

His boots lost traction on the wet rock, forcing him into a half-crawl. He inched forward, the lantern's plastic handle clenched between his teeth. The rugged floor tore and stung his bare hands. Still, it was less precarious than walking upright. A haunting image of his potential fall repeated: his head bashed in, blood mixing hazily with water, the pink stream trickling through Nausi's worksite unnoticed. Just as his jaw started aching from the lantern's weight, its twinkle faded. In the impenetrable darkness, he recalled picking it up off the work bench, where it had sat, inches away from its charger. He debated his options: slide back down into what may be an entirely flooded tunnel or keep climbing upslope, sight unseen, toward the world.

In the absence of visual stimulus, Simón's mind filled the void, flashing at random. The vibrant green of Terrance's stir-fried snow peas, electric magenta of Roberta's hair, cold gray of his mother's composite floor. Stone snagged the fabric of his backpack; he stopped, feeling the increasingly tight contours of the surrounding space. Nausi was right: it was getting narrow. He flattened himself against the wet rock, boots scrabbling for friction, working him forward.

An idea rattled him. *I have all the space I need.*

He shimmied the backpack's straps over his shoulders,

wiggling forward like a molting snake, the tunnel's rough surface freeing him from the burden. He marveled as it vanished behind him.

Faster now. Swimming in the community center pool, bony chest near bursting. Faster now. Biking through Echo Bend in the early days of spring. Faster now. On the way to that married man's palatial house for the first time, aroused by the danger and the promise.

A neon glow illuminated ahead. He stopped to rub his eyes, to make sure it was actually there. No matter which way he turned his head, the light remained. His heart pounded with possibility, and he skittered toward it, famished. The closer he got, the wider the tunnel opened, until there was just enough room to stand. Before him, the green glow faded into full spectrum color.

How the granite flesh bent and twisted, molten body sinuating before Simón's eyes. He no longer heard the water. Only the great earth mutating. The walls themselves undressed their black carapace — to tremendous paintings of foxglove and beebalm, sun-teeming hills, and forested waterfalls. Wildernesses, impossibly alive in the aftermath of summer. Above, on the stone ceiling, another sprawling mural of aurora borealis: whirling feathers of cosmic green, teal, violet. Symbolized in color, a vast shared language.

Swift now, his limbs loosened. He walked toward the wall, where a gold-framed door with a window waited.

He reached out but found no knob. The door wouldn't budge when pushed. He peered through the window, into an outdated bathroom.

A dark-haired man gripped a camera like a handgun, eye pressed to the hammer. "Now swim," he said. The voice, familiar, but smooth with youth. *Abi,* Simón wanted to cry out, but he held his tongue, unwilling to interrupt the artist at work. He peered over the edge of the tub, expecting to see his mother's yellow swimsuit. But in her place, three battered pigeons flapped and sputtered, splashing dark bloody water onto pink mid-century tiles. He stepped closer, squinted. The water had stained the birds' whitest feathers purple. Not blood at all, he realized. Wine.

Artifice.

The words were clear as day. But the man in the bathroom hadn't said them.

I'm over here. ¡Apúrate!

"What?" He turned to the muraled wall with the knob-less door. A tall, artful willow tree seemed to vibrate atop its hill, ebullient against the motionless landscape.

Artifice. It means someone decided what was real, and what wasn't. It means nothing here can hurt you.

Simón glanced around, from the tree to the door and back again. His mind was playing tricks on him.

Don't bother with the bathroom. There's no getting in. The painted tree's leaves fluttered in the breeze.

"I don't wanna get in," Simón said. "I want to get out."

The willow's brown bark shivered, verdant branches buffeting in the brush-stroked wind. Its words were comforting, carrying the familiar sadness of reuniting with an old friend.

I can help you, said the willow. *You just have to let me.*

Guided by some unknown force, Simón stepped closer to the mural, lifting his bloodied palm to the tree's whisky-brown trunk. Every breath left his lungs.

It wasn't cold like stone. It was warm. Warm, like someone's chest; rising, falling, rising, falling. Warm like sunburst spewing out between fat, dark clouds.

Nothing here can hurt you.

Tears welled and spilled over. He took a deep breath, then pushed. Dazzling light enveloped him as everything fell away — the panic over his career, the uncertainty around his malformed relationships, the unfinished artworks — all meaningless in the realm of nothing.

Am I dead?

Far from it, the willow told him. *Now, leap.*

Color flooded back into the frame. Vivid, wheeling fractals faded below him: the real, green world. He felt strong, lighter in body.

He dipped toward the yellowing foliage, the ash, the oak, the pine, the willow; then, overcome by instinct, twisted his shoulders forward to slow mid descent. Armfuls of sky, every breath tasted like petrichor. The winding paths dancing in wildflower, the gray and gleaming ponds; the chipmunk in the hickory, the toad below the wineberry, the spiders in the ivy, the monarchs among the plume: familiar. He passed over a cluster of khaki-clad beasts with black binoculars for eyes, all but one gazing up at him: a brown-skinned woman in pine-green, spinning and searching for something, someone, at ground-level.

He was pulled, magnetic, to a nearby copse of trees. Passing over, a clearing, and at its center, a pale, lost man lifting a microphone to the sky, wincing as though battered by invisible rain.

Simón opened his mouth and sang.

Acknowledgments

Thank you to the following musical artists and/or their listed works, alluded to throughout *Spark Bird*. These fellow creators and these referenced albums continue to inspire us as artists, while also expressing our characters' inner worlds:

Stars of the Lid – The Tired Sounds of Stars of the Lid

Hiroshi Yoshimura – Wet Land

Brian Eno – Ambient 1: Music for Airports

Paul Simon – Rhythm of the Saints

Talk Talk – Spirit of Eden

Jon Hassell – Dream Theory in Malaya: Fourth World Vol. Two

SOPHIE – Oil of Every Pearl's Un-Insides

Susumu Yokota – Acid Mt. Fuji

The Mars Volta – Deloused in the Comatorium

Harold Budd – The Pavilion of Dreams

The Congos – Heart of the Congos

Constance Demby - Novus Magnificat

Angelo Badalamenti & Julee Cruise – Soundtrack of *Twin Peaks*

Additional thanks to the following: Sufjan Stevens, Explosions in the Sky, Aphex Twin, Miles Davis, Antonio Vivaldi, Mary J. Blige, Julien Gracq, William Shakespeare, Hayao Miyazaki, and Edmund Spenser.

Endless gratitude to those who read earlier versions of this manuscript, and shared invaluable insights during the process. We give our dearest thanks and attribute this book's existence to the following: Josh Dale, Kat Giordano, and Maddy Brozusky for their direction and support. To Delana Listman, Chrissy DeRock, and Zach Ozma for their love, patience, and understanding while we tirelessly completed this novel. To Thirty West Publishing for gifting the spark to ignite our flame, lending us the trust and resources to create *Spark Bird*, and for publishing it to be widely read. To Jenn Zed for granting us artwork that is both portentous and meditative, both looming and consoling.

Most of all, to our readers who we dearly cherish: thank you for allowing us this space and thank you for giving it your time and attention.

About The Author

Jonathan Koven lives in Philadelphia with his wife Delana and their two cats Peanut Butter and Keebler. He works as a technical writer and reads poetry manuscripts for Moonstone Arts. A Pushcart Prize nominee, Jonathan has both fiction and poetry published by Assure Press, Animal Heart Press, *300 Days of Sun*, and more. He is the author of the poetry chapbook *Palm Lines* (2020), the award-winning fiction novella, *Below Torrential Hill* (2021), and the poetry collection, *Mystic Orchards* (2023).

About The Author

Daniel DeRock is a writer from the U.S. living in the Netherlands. You can find his stories in *Pithead Chapel, Gone Lawn, MoonPark Review, and Ligeia Magazine,* among other outlets. His work has been nominated for the Pushcart Prize, Best of the Net, and Best Microfiction. He is a co-editor of *Icebreakers Lit,* an online magazine for collaborative writing. For publications and more, see danielderock.com

About The Author

Julian Shendelman lives with his husband and dogs near Philadelphia. His poetry chapbook, "Dead Dad Club," was published by Nomadic Press in 2017 and his prose has appeared in Bat City Review, Philadelphia Stories, and Cleaver Magazine. He is currently working on a novel about haunted houses, capitalism, and community. Learn more at www.shendelman.com

About the Publisher

Follow us on:

Scan the QR code to visit us

www.thirtywestph.com